Praise for

THE SELFISH GIANT

"Jacob is a very successful lawyer. He prides himself on being a self-made man, and as it is said, 'Pride goeth before the fall.' What is really important in life? What happens to the ones we love when our inflated ego runs rampant? Is the path to spirituality paved with pain? In this soulful story, Berkley fearlessly explores these key life questions. *The Selfish Giant* is ultimately a tale of hope, and second chances. It's well worth the price of admission."

—John J Jessop
Author of *Pleasuria: Take as Directed, Murder by Road Trip, Guardian Angel: Unforgiven, Guardian Angel, Indoctrination*

"A powerful story about redemption, ambitions, and family, *The Selfish Giant* is a must-read. Benjamin Berkley takes readers on a dark journey of many twists, turns, and lessons learned."

—Swati Singh
Author of *Her Brave Journey*

"When Jacob, patriarch of a dysfunctional family and a hard-charging attorney, meets a stranger on a beach in Hawaii, his life is changed forever. And not necessarily for the better."

—Betsy Ashton
Suspense Author of the Award-Winning *Betrayal*

"Attorney Jacob Abrams undergoes cardiac rehabilitation, and the process is more spiritual than medical. In *The Selfish Giant*, Benjamin Berkley tells a captivating tale of a cold-blooded man finding his heart, rich with details of family life, faith development, and personal transformation."

—Henry G. Brinton
Author of *City of Peace* and *Windows of the Heavens*

The Selfish Giant

By Benjamin H. Berkley

Published by

köehlerbooks™

3705 Shore Drive
Virginia Beach, VA 23455
800–435–4811
www.koehlerbooks.com

THE SELFISH GIANT

BENJAMIN H. BERKLEY

VIRGINIA BEACH
CAPE CHARLES

Dedication:

To Riley, my furry best friend.
He enriched our lives with love and sweetness.
May his memory be a blessing.

T he Selfish Giant portrays a fictional, maskless post-pandemic world. And represents our hopes for the future.

The global spread of the Covid-19 pandemic at the beginning of 2020 brought radical changes to the lifestyle of millions of people, including abrupt restrictions to our freedom to roam. The strict limitations to the places we could inhabit and visit gave way to the yearning for the places where we wanted to be.

In March 2020, the world changed further as social distancing measures and stay-at-home rules were implemented in multiple countries around the globe as a response to the pandemic. Personal geographies shrank to the spaces within the walls of a home, the route taken to the local supermarket, or the distance that could be traveled on foot or bicycle within the space of an allotted exercise hour. We made friends with our neighbors, had drive-by birthday parties, and pedaled in place up the steepest mountains while our kitchen tables became offices and schools.

But the one thing that the pandemic has not impaired is our ability to imagine. At first, to imagine those places we had been from memory. And later, to create in our minds new alternative worlds, bucket lists, and a true utopia.

Imagination is the most powerful and wonderful tool we have. Never stop imagining. It is our window into the future.

CHAPTER ONE

P ositioned directly above a narrow, rectangular table, the circular light flickered, and the room took on an intense white brightness. Wearing blue surgical masks and surgical gowns, ten faces assumed their assigned positions while an equal number of trained faces looked down from an observation window above.

"Just checking your bracelet, Jacob. Want to make sure it's you. "

Jacob struggled to open his eyes as his left hand was raised and turned. Draped in only a pale-green sheet, Jacob rested motionless with his arms crossed on a table too small for his body.

"Sure don't want you suing us, Jacob."

The masked dozen produced a weak laugh. And as Jacob rolled his head from side to side, the laughter was quickly replaced by the pumping sound of air being squeezed through a tube and released.

Another voice is heard. "All right, Jacob. Time to go to sleep. I am going to ask you to count backwards from one hundred. Okay?"

Jacob nodded and slightly raised his head, straining to read the time on the clock on the wall. A middle-aged woman with long gray hair wearing street clothes was standing near the clock. Appearing over her head was a soft glow. Motioning with her hand to her mouth, she sent a kiss to Jacob, which comforted him as he lay back and received a clear mask over his mouth and nose. The mask turned cloudy as he softly spoke.

"One hundred, ninety-nine, ninety-eight . . ."

CHAPTER TWO

Slowly and carefully, Jacob toddled along the dirt path that led from his backyard to the man-made lake below. A year ago, before he became ill, Jacob could walk around the lake in twenty minutes. Now, with a portable oxygen pack strapped to his waist, he shuffled to the closest bench, steps away from the calm water of the lake. Out of breath, he sat, his lanky frame hunched from the effort of walking.

At six foot nine, Jacob used to be a commanding presence. Now his skin hung loose on him, the sign of too much weight lost too quickly, and his skin was clammy. He had been overweight and unhealthy before, but now, with a heart that seemed determined to fail, Jacob looked like what he was—a man on the edge of death.

He watched as a man a little older than his own fifty-one years approached, tossing a toddler into the air and catching him again. The little boy laughed for joy.

"Good looking grandson," Jacob commented.

"Thanks. They're a lot of fun. But the best part is, when you get tired, you give them back to their parents."

"So I have heard," Jacob said, smiling.

Taking a deep breath while adjusting the oxygen cannula, Jacob gazed at the grandfather and little boy as they continued their walk around the lake.

"That could have been me," he mused.

"Hey, mister. What is that belt around your waist for?" a curly-haired boy no more than eight asked Jacob. He had a backpack and was getting ready to cast his fishing line into the water.

"It helps me breathe."

"Why do you need help breathing?" the boy asked as he cast out his line.

"Well, I have a bad ticker. My heart. I am waiting for the doctors to give me a new heart. Have you caught anything?"

"Nope."

"Well, fishing requires that you have a lot of patience. Fishing is all about patience."

"My dad is a doctor, and he has lots of patients."

Jacob laughed. It felt good to laugh; it had been too long.

"It sounds the same but means something else," he explained. "It's a virtue."

"What's a virtue?"

"Something that took me way too long to learn."

The boy looked at him warily. "I don't know, mister. I just want to catch a fish," he said, reeling in his line and darting away.

Tired but not quite ready to go back to the house, Jacob reached for a small packet of seeds in his pocket. He tossed some into the lake, and as if on cue, a duck sporting a purple-and-yellow neck approached, gobbling up the seeds.

"Hey, Laker. Where have you been? We need to talk. The boys have lost two in a row. And we have only four games left to play."

Jacob tossed Laker a few seeds. "And I don't think I am going to live long enough to see the playoffs."

Laker spun around as if he understood. Jacob leaned forward and spoke confidentially. "We've talked before about this, but I'm worried about how Gail is going to take it when I'm gone. I know Nicole and Aaron will do their best to be there for her, but they have a new baby now, so they will be busy. Every time I try to talk about what to do when I'm gone, Gail starts crying. It breaks my heart, which you know is funny, because my heart is pretty bad already."

The duck quacked, and Jacob laughed shakily. "Yeah, okay, bad joke. It's just that I think I have finally learned what I was doing wrong all those years, and I worry it's too late to put that lesson to use now. But it is not in my hands. And tonight, we have my first grandchild's bris. I am so proud and so afraid. Oh, Laker, how did I get here?"

CHAPTER THREE

One year ago

Dr. Lowy's waiting room needed updating. The dark-brown chairs lining the three walls of the square room were badly scuffed, and there were footprint tracks on the carpet. Jacob Abrams, the self-proclaimed "most ruthless lawyer in LA," decided he would say something to his friend and doctor. No sense in letting the doctor embarrass himself by keeping a tired office. Wouldn't he want it to be the best?

Jacob walked up to the receptionist's window to announce his arrival.

"I have a five o'clock appointment."

Holding up her index finger to signal that she would be right with him, the receptionist continued to take a patient's details over the phone.

"Excuse me," Jacob interrupted.

Placing her caller on hold, the receptionist kindly requested that Jacob take a seat.

"Why should I? Tell Dr. Lowy that I'm here," Jacob said.

"Dr. Lowy is in with a patient, but I will buzz him when he is done," the receptionist said patiently. "I'll just finish up this call, and then I'll be able to assist you. Please do take a seat."

Huffing, Jacob stalked over to one of the chairs and squeezed his large body into it. The tight fit annoyed him. The receptionist not knowing who he was annoyed him. Grabbing a *Sports Illustrated* off the glass-topped table next to him, Jacob fanned his face with the magazine and loosened his tie.

"It's hot in here. Aren't you hot?" Jacob said loudly. The other patient in the waiting room studiously avoided his gaze and kept her eyes glued to the phone in her hand. The receptionist ignored his question, continuing her phone call. Jacob tried to shift his weight, but the arms of the chair acted like a vise and kept him in place. When did chairs get so small?

"Mr. Abrams," the receptionist said, hanging up her phone, "just sign in here. And I need you to update your medical history. I also need to take a picture of your health insurance card."

Gripping the base on the chair, Jacob launched himself out of the seat and charged the receptionist's window like a rhino.

"I don't need to fill out anything," he barked. "I am a friend of Dr. Lowy's."

"Mr. Abrams, I understand," the receptionist said, her voice wavering under the fierce glare of his brown eyes. Jacob noticed her name tag read *Cindy*. "But your medication may have changed, or something else. I am just doing my job as Dr. Lowy has requested that I do." She tried to hand Jacob a pen, but he refused to take it.

"You're new?" he said, bearing down on her as if she were a witness in court.

"I am. I've been here about three months," she replied.

"Well, I have known your boss for over twenty-five years," Jacob said haughtily. Cindy put the pen down and tried to look away, but Jacob kept talking. "Could you please check how much longer Dr. Lowy is going to be?" he said condescendingly.

"I'm sorry, but Dr. Lowy had two emergencies today and is running late," Cindy said, holding her chin up.

"Well, I am running out of patience."

Just then, a cheerful voice reached them from the hallway. "Cindy will set you up for a checkup."

As the door swung open, George Lowy appeared, ushering a patient out. He wore a doctor's white coat with a stethoscope wrapped around the collar. He was a little older than Jacob, in his mid-fifties, and Jacob noticed with satisfaction that the doctor's curly black hair was going gray more quickly than Jacob's own brown hair.

Dr. Lowy extended his hand to shake. "Come on back, Jacob. Sorry to keep you waiting."

As the two men walked in single file to the examination room, Jacob asked, "Are you really sorry?"

"Excuse me?" Dr. Lowy paused. "I got behind. It happens. Sorry."

"Well, had I known, I would have booked another appointment and made some money instead of having to make bullshit chitchat with your staff! By the way, that waiting room is looking tired. You should get it redone," Jacob said. He saw Dr. Lowy's shoulders stiffen.

Once in the examination room, Dr. Lowy grabbed Jacob's chart from a shelf hanging on the door.

"Take your shirt off and sit down on the table," Lowy said as he reviewed the chart. "Oh, I see you and Cindy got off to a great start. You refused to fill out my forms."

"Waste of time."

"Really. For whom?"

Jacob didn't bother answering. He removed his white shirt and tie, noticing with annoyance that his tie had a small mustard stain from lunch.

"Did you go to law school?" Dr. Lowy asked. "Well, somewhere along the way you must have learned about following procedures. Obeying rules."

"What are you talking about?"

"Do you think you are above the law? Better than everyone else? We have rules in my office. Patients fill out our forms. And if patients don't want to comply, I can't help them."

"You are really too much," Jacob said, rolling his eyes.

Dr. Lowy folded his hands in front of him. "All right. Do you want me to examine you?"

"No. But my wife does."

"Smart woman." Dr. Lowy paused. "Look, Jacob. We're friends. But I am tired. I started rounds today at 6 a.m. and I would like to go home, have dinner, and watch the news before I start all over again tomorrow. So, if you do not mind, be a good boy, take off your undershirt, and let me examine you."

"You're the doctor," Jacob said, voice dripping with sarcasm. "And you make the rules." He had to tug a few times to free his undershirt from his large belly, then pulled the shirt over his head.

Dr. Lowy took his blood pressure and listened to his heartbeat and made notes in Jacob's chart. Then he put the chart down and scrutinized Jacob.

"Are you still smoking?"

Jacob glanced to the side but didn't speak. He'd thought the mints had covered up the smell.

"I will take that as a yes," Dr. Lowy said sourly. "All right, next topic. You know you're fat."

"Wow, Doc. Whatever happened to a doctor's bedside manner?" Jacob retorted.

"You are so right, Jacob," Dr. Lowy said with exaggerated contrition. "What was I thinking? You are morbidly obese. That sounds better. Now please stand up."

Jacob got to his feet with a little difficulty.

"Touch your toes. Oh wait, you can't. Because you can't even see your toes." Dr. Lowy made another note in the chart and then walked to the door. "All right. Get dressed. We'll talk in my office."

A lot of trouble for a cold stethoscope and scratchy Velcro blood pressure cuff, Jacob thought. He put his clothes back on and joined Dr. Lowy in his office.

Three mugs, all with varying levels of now cold coffee, were scattered on Dr. Lowy's untidy desk. Behind Dr. Lowy, the wood-paneled wall held the doctor's medical school degree and many awards for charitable work.

"Very impressive," Jacob said as he entered the room, gesturing to the "wall of honors" with his chin.

"You say that every time you're here," Dr. Lowy said, not looking up from the chart in front of him.

"I do?" Jacob feigned ignorance.

"Don't kid me, Jacob. You are the most calculated person I know. Take a seat."

Jacob eased into the chair in front of the desk, grateful that it didn't have arms to constrict him.

"How long have we known each other?" Dr. Lowy asked as he flipped through his chart notes.

"We met when the kids were very little. Indian Princesses. We both joined at the same time," Jacob remembered.

"That's right, although they call them 'Adventure Guides' now, I guess to be politically correct. And how long have I been your doctor?"

"George. Where are you going with this?" Jacob asked impatiently.

"Have you ever taken my advice?" Jacob didn't dignify that with a response. "Look," Dr. Lowy said, "I know you're the lion in the courtroom. But here, I roar. Jacob, your cholesterol is way up. Your triglycerides are off the chart. Your blood pressure is at stroke level. You eat crap and drink too much. I know because Susie and I have been out with you and Gail. And how was that hot dog you had for lunch?" Jacob winced. "What, you thought I didn't see the stain on your tie?" Jacob unconsciously brushed his hand against the stain.

Dr. Lowy continued, "I don't know, Jacob. If we weren't friends, I would not be talking this frankly. But we are. And you can't keep on going like this. Just because you're taller, that does not mean your heart is larger. It just has to pump harder."

Jacob looked at his watch, a trick he'd learned in the courtroom, to unnerve his opponent and get him to wrap up.

"Do you have to be somewhere?" Dr. Lowy asked, one eyebrow raised. "Oh, another thing, you were supposed to quit smoking."

"I also thought someday I would play for the Lakers," Jacob said. "But that's not happening either."

"Go ahead. Make jokes," Dr. Lowy said, shaking his head. Then he tried another tactic. "You know, Gail is very attractive. She will have no problem meeting someone new. Is that what you want? Your wife sleeping in your bed with someone else?"

Jacob felt his cheeks getting red. *Fight fire with fire*, he thought, and he said out loud, "Are you expressing an interest, Dr. Lowy?"

Talking a deep breath, Dr. Lowy continued. "It is not all about you. And besides, even if you don't want to take care of yourself, you should consider how it might affect Gail."

"I have that covered. My finances are good," Jacob said. "Anything else, Doctor?"

"I'm increasing your blood pressure and cholesterol medication. And you need to lose fifty pounds. That would be a good start."

"I walk," Jacob protested.

"Not enough. You need to do more. Something for your heart *and* your soul. I have a great program, and you'll get some exercise. Every Sunday, me and a couple of other guys from the temple, you probably know them, we go to the local grocery stores and restaurants, and they give us their unsold food. It's only going to get thrown out. We take it to a food bank. It's fun. And you'll feel good."

"Well, you keep that fun to yourself," Jacob said dismissively.

"Seriously, do you ever volunteer? Do you ever give back? What is it called for lawyers? Pro bono."

"I leave all that volunteering stuff up to my, as you say, very attractive wife. That way she can meet guys at the same time." *There, that should shut him up.*

It did seem to work. Dr. Lowy sighed and reached for the prescription pad in his coat pocket.

"I'm giving you another prescription. Read it once a day for thirty days and then call me. You need to fill it right away." He scribbled a note and handed it to Jacob.

"What's this? Your handwriting is terrible."

"*The Selfish Giant.* It's a book. And remember, charity begins with the heart."

CHAPTER FOUR

Jacob ignored Cindy's friendly "good night" on his way out of Dr. Lowy's office. As he squeezed into his car, he muttered to himself, "What, he thinks he's a rabbi now as well as a doctor, and he can lecture me on charity? Stick to your day job, George."

Peeling out of the car park, Jacob tuned in to the Lakers game and lit up a cigarette, then ripped open a bag of M&Ms. He rolled down his window and breathed in the muggy night air.

Traffic wasn't too bad, and it wasn't long before he was exiting the freeway and slowing down for the red stoplight at the intersection. Out of the corner of his eye, he saw a man with an unkempt beard and ripped jeans approach his car. The man's ragged cardboard sign read, *Will Work For $$*.

"If that were true, you'd get a job," Jacob grumbled. He pushed the button to roll up the window and with his other hand flipped the beggar the bird. The man winced slightly and moved on, searching for a more compassionate driver. Before he had disappeared in the side mirror, Jacob had already forgotten him. The light turned green, and as he drove on, he only thought about whether the Lakers' defense was up to the challenge tonight.

Jacob and Gail lived in a gated community. Jacob was still proud of how he'd gotten the house for less than asking price—"by ten grand!" he'd brag every time he mentioned it at a cocktail party. But his favorite part about living there wasn't the huge house but rather the little lake in the community park. His chats with Laker the duck were often the only times he felt like he could breathe. He wasn't fighting anyone or proving anything, just sitting by a lake, and chatting with a duck. Not that he'd ever admit this to anybody. Jacob Abrams was a shark. Sharks don't need rest.

Jacob entered his code at the gates and impatiently drove through as soon as there was just enough room to do so. He tossed his empty bag of M&Ms in the back and threw his smoldering cigarette butt out of the window, roaring down the street. A neighbor looked up from her evening gardening, startled by the noise. Jacob laughed rudely and drove on.

He let the door slam behind him, puffing a little from the effort of climbing the two stairs from the garage to the kitchen. The fact that this made him out of breath annoyed him and reminded him of his conversation with Dr. Lowy, which annoyed him further. He watched Gail at the kitchen island, pouring pasta out of a steaming pot while talking on her cell phone, and tried to be less annoyed. He didn't want to start the evening on a bad note.

"Dad's home. I'll call you later," Gail said to Nicole on the phone. She ended the call as Jacob pecked her on the cheek, brushing her stylish blonde hair back as she set the pot down. He was about to ask how their daughter was, but Gail turned to him and immediately asked, "So, what did George say?"

Jacob stiffened and stumped over to the desk in the living room. *So much for not being annoyed.* He put his attaché case on the desk chair and bent down to scratch Riley the cat's head.

"How about starting with 'Hello, how was your day? How much money did you make to keep me in my lifestyle?'" he demanded.

"Hello. What did Dr. Lowy say?" Gail asked, undeterred.

"He said I'm not getting laid enough," Jacob said.

"Really! Perhaps he should talk to me so I can explain," Gail retorted. Jacob kept his head down and his gaze on Riley so she couldn't see the look of shame that crossed his face. He knew he hadn't been an attentive lover in a while.

"Did you feed him? He's acting like he's still hungry," Jacob said, petting his cat's luxurious coat of fur.

"Yes," Gail said impatiently. "Now, are you going to tell me what George said?"

Jacob unbent himself with a small groan, holding his hand to his back as he creaked into a standing position. "Well, the great doctor said I needed to lose weight. Imagine that. Twelve fucking years of med school and he just figured out that I need to lose weight!"

"What else?"

"The usual," Jacob said, waving his hand dismissively. "Can we eat?"

"Be ready in a minute," Gail replied, shaking the water out of the pasta in a colander. Jacob went to the refrigerator and took out a salami for a pre-dinner snack. Setting the colander down, Gail stepped over and took the cured meat out of his hand, saying, "You are like a child. Go sit down."

Riley hopped up on the seat next to Jacob, and Jacob massaged the top of his head again. Gail brought over two plates. As she set them down, Jacob stared down at the small serving of a plain-looking meal. He frowned.

"What is this?"

"Strips of roasted chicken over a multigrain pasta," she said, sitting and unfolding her napkin to place on her lap.

"It looks disgusting."

"Thank you so much," Gail said. She took a deep breath and

changed the subject. "Did you see the news? All of those poor people who lost their homes in the floods."

"Idiots," Jacob said through a mouthful of pasta.

"What?"

"They're idiots. That river floods every year, and those idiots stay there. They deserve what they get." Jacob glanced up from his food and saw a cast of surprised sadness flit across his wife's face. He couldn't imagine why she felt that way; he was just telling the truth.

Jacob reached for the saltshaker, but Gail grabbed his hand before he could lift it.

"George called me," Gail said.

"Then why did you ask how it went?" Jacob growled.

"I just wanted to see what you would say," she replied softly. Jacob reached again for the saltshaker, and this time Gail used both hands to stop him. "Seriously, Jacob. You need to take control of your health, and it is my job to make sure you do it." Jacob withdrew his hand.

"How much you getting paid? Whatever it is, I'll double it if you come work for me. It's more fun," he groused. Gail moved the saltshaker further away as Jacob took another bite of healthy pasta. Swallowing, he made a face.

"I heard some sad news," Gail said, pressing on with conversation.

"What?"

"Jack Singer died."

"Who?"

"Lorraine's husband. You've met him. He does financial planning. We sat with them at the Federation dinner. They are friends with the Bermans.

"Oh yeah, I think I remember," Jacob acknowledged. He tried to show some interest. "Was he sick?"

"Colon cancer. They kept it quiet. She still has two boys in college," Gail said sorrowfully.

"I remember now. He was a prick," Jacob pronounced.

"Why do you say that?" Gail asked.

"I don't know. He probably was." Jacob didn't know why he did this, why he insisted on being contrary and saying things that made Gail uncomfortable. He loved her, but she seemed to always be thinking about other people and worrying about their welfare. It didn't get her anywhere, just made her sad about their problems. Why should he have to do the same? He had his own problems. He swallowed another bite of the tasteless pasta and said deliberately, "And his wife's cute. Very skinny. Tight ass. She'll have no problem."

"You're disgusting," Gail said, and Jacob was a little ashamed of the thrill of victory he felt, having achieved the reaction he was going for.

"What? That's what a woman has to do," Jacob forged ahead. "If she has kids in school and a mortgage to pay, and she is not working, and her husband did not do a good job of financial planning, how else is she going to pay for things unless she . . ." He trailed off as Gail shook her head, her lips pressed together in a tight line.

They ate in silence for a few minutes. Jacob's mind drifted to a client he had seen earlier that day, and he was turning over in his mind a technically difficult part of that case when Gail suddenly spoke again.

"Roslyn called. They wanted to know if we would take out an ad for the annual temple dinner dance. They're honoring Steve and Sherri Rosen," she said.

"What did you tell her?" Jacob asked, trying to pull his mind back from work to what he saw as the mundane.

"I said yes, of course," Gail replied in a surprised tone.

"Well, tell her no," Jacob snapped. He worked hard every damn day, and he was expected to just give that money away to anyone who asked.

"I sent the check this afternoon," Gail said. She moved a piece of chicken around on her plate with her fork and said quietly, "Anyway, I don't want to be the richest person in the cemetery."

Jacob snorted and took a big gulp from his water glass. "You don't have to worry about that. I will be there long before you." He knew what she meant, but he refused to feel bad about wanting to keep the money he had rightfully earned. Gail shook her head.

"So, how was your day?" she asked as she stabbed the piece of chicken she'd been playing with.

"Great. I shook down this client for five thousand," Jacob boasted.

"Shook down?"

"This guy came whimpering into my office like a schoolgirl. Cops charged him with peeing on the side of the road. He went through a whole box of Kleenex. So, I gave him the snow job that he is probably facing jail but I could keep him out, for the low, low price of five thousand. He whipped out his credit card." Jacob laughed at the memory. "Easy money. It will take me ten minutes. What a jerk! Could have taken care of it himself." Jacob chuckled again and then caught the look Gail was giving him. "What?"

"Are you looking for a response?" she asked. "I don't know what to say." She took a drink of water, and Jacob shoved the last of the pasta into his mouth, annoyed that his amusing story had tanked so badly. *She could take more pride in my accomplishments*, he thought. She wouldn't be ungrateful for that $5,000 the next time she went shopping, for crying out loud.

Once again, Gail changed the subject, and once again, she hit on a sore spot.

"I saw Diane today. She was at the nail shop."

Jacob bristled. "That must have been awkward."

"It was. Considering we're not talking to her or Michael, and yet they are the parents of our son-in-law."

"How long are you going to keep bringing this up to me?" Jacob complained.

"What you did was wrong," Gail said firmly.

"Well, we'll see if the judge agrees with you," Jacob said, pushing his chair back and standing from the table.

"It's hurting our daughter's relationship with her husband," Gail continued, as she too stood and started gathering the dishes.

"How so?"

"You are not nice to Aaron. And it's obvious. He did nothing wrong. The problem is between you and Michael. You love Aaron, and it's not fair to punish him just because you picked a fight with his father."

Riley jumped on the table, and Jacob bent to pick him up. This was such a familiar refrain he could have repeated it in his sleep. Each time Gail brought it up, Jacob dug in deeper, refusing to change his mind about something that as far as he was concerned was a matter of history. He and his law partner had parted ways, and they were still sorting out who owed what to whom. Why dwell?

"As a means of making amends, because you know you treat Aaron badly, Nicole is going to invite you over tomorrow to watch the game with Aaron," Gail said, changing the tune slightly.

"I don't need my daughter making playdates for me," Jacob said. He carried Riley into the living room and sat in his favorite armchair, picking up the TV remote.

"Be nice," Gail admonished. She finished clearing the table by herself.

Jacob turned up the volume on the TV.

CHAPTER FIVE

Nicole pressed the heels of her hands to her temples. Why did she feel a headache coming on right now? Maybe she needed more water. As she filled a glass at the sink, she realized with a start that the headache had started as soon as her mom had said "Dad's home." Why was that?

As she checked the chicken roasting in the oven, Nicole admitted to herself that she knew the reason why. Her dad had always been a bit difficult to get to know, a little rough around the edges, but lately it was harder to bear. It seemed every time she talked to her mom now, she had to listen to a litany of complaints about her dad. She felt awkward hearing these things, like she was eavesdropping where she didn't belong, but her mom didn't seem to find anything odd with it, and she shared each time Jacob was rude to a waiter or bragged about driving a hard bargain at work or saving money on a purchase. With every misdeed or unkind word Gail repeated, Nicole's heart grew heavier.

Nicole had always worshiped her dad. He was a giant to her from a young age, not just due to his great height and broad shoulders, perfect for piggyback rides, but because he always seemed to know what he was doing. He was so sure of himself, and Nicole, a naturally shy child, found this almost miraculous. Where did he get that sense that he could take up space, that the world owed him good things, and that he could complain if the world didn't deliver? Conversely, Nicole could hardly bear to correct her fifth-grade teacher when the woman announced the wrong day for Nicole's class birthday; she couldn't imagine negotiating thousands of dollars off the price of a house or demanding outrageously biased plea deals for clients.

Maybe even more miraculously, Jacob thought the same rules applied to her. If he was entitled to the best, so was she. She deserved the best of everything, from the house she grew up in to the school she attended, from the clothes she wore to the vacations she went on. By the same token, he expected the best of her. She had to get straight As, she had to be first violin in the school orchestra, she had to make varsity on the track team. She never resented this, though; she saw how hard he worked at his job and figured the same principle applied to her. She deserved the best, but she had to work hard for it.

And now she had the best, didn't she? Nicole poured herself a glass of wine and sat at the kitchen island. She was working her way up the ladder at her hedge fund company, she was married to a successful lawyer, lived in a very nice home in a very nice neighborhood, could name the designer for almost everything she was wearing, and recently returned from a week at an exclusive resort in the Caribbean. By any measure, she was doing well, and all this at only age twenty-five.

And her dad was doing well too, of course. The house, the boat, the fancy car. But more and more it sounded like he didn't think it was enough. Nicole had always assumed he thought hard work and good things went hand in hand, but lately she wondered if he felt entitled to the benefits without the effort, or if he thought working hard when he was younger meant he didn't have to try anymore. Was that why he sounded so bitter when he talked about work, or why he left all the charitable giving to Gail?

Also, she had to admit that her father wasn't doing well in everything. Her mom's call just now had been mostly about how he had gone to see Dr. Lowy today and she was worried about what the doctor would say. Her dad had gained so much weight in the last few years. Nicole glanced at a photo of the two of them at her wedding just two and a half years ago, where he was noticeably slimmer. Her mother fretted about her father's health, and on Dr. Lowy's advice, she was trying out a new recipe tonight that had all the low-fat, low-cholesterol ingredients her dad should be having. She knew her Jacob would hate it, and she'd expressed her worry about it to Nicole. Nicole spent quite some time reassuring her mother that her father would like it, or at least pretend to like it because her mother had gone to the trouble of making it.

The oven timer dinged, and Nicole got up to take the chicken out. As she set her wineglass down, she noticed it was empty. Hadn't she just poured a glass? How quickly had she drunk that? She frowned. She didn't think of herself as a heavy drinker, or as thoughtlessly gluttonous. Where had that impulse come from?

Twenty minutes later, she ladled vegetables onto the plates and set them on the table, just as the garage door closed. *Perfect timing*, she thought.

"Hi, honey," she said as Aaron entered the kitchen, amorously kissing him on the lips.

"Hi yourself," he said, swatting her backside.

"Aaron!" she laughed. "Stop that silliness and sit down. Let's eat while it's still hot."

"I love that you're still making me dinners," Aaron said, sitting. "Lucky for me you're an insane morning person and go in to work at 7 a.m."

"It's easier to get things done when the office is quiet," Nicole explained. "And you know I find cooking relaxing. This way, I get to have it all."

"Why compromise when you can get everything you want, right?"

"I don't mean it like that," Nicole protested.

"I know you don't, hon. I was just joking," Aaron reassured her. "Hey, this chicken is really good. What did you do to it?"

"I marinated it overnight. It's a new recipe.

"Well, I really like it. Let's add it to the list of regulars."

"Okay," Nicole said happily. She liked cooking for its own sake because she found it relaxing, but she couldn't deny that she also liked the praise she got for doing it well.

"We had the farewell party for Sharon today," Aaron said tentatively.

"Oh?" Nicole said, feeling herself tense up.

"Yeah, we took up a donation and got her one of those Stokke strollers, so she was happy about that."

"I can imagine. Those things are expensive."

"Yeah. Not that she'll be able to use it for the first few weeks. She is unlikely to leave the house, isn't she?"

"How do you mean?"

"Just that newborns only eat and poop and sleep. Sharon will be too tired to go out anywhere."

"Yes, well. I'm sure when she does, she will appreciate having that stroller," Nicole said.

"Yes." Aaron cleared his throat and reached for his water glass. Nicole took a couple deep breaths and consciously changed the subject.

"So, tomorrow's the big day. Are you ready for this?"

"Yeah, I can do it. It'll take a couple beers, but I'll get through it."

Nicole reached out to put a hand over Aaron's. He looked into her eyes, and they smiled at one another.

"You're a good man, Aaron," Nicole said.

Aaron brought Nicole's hand to his mouth and kissed it.

"Anything for you," he said.

CHAPTER SIX

Nearly finished clearing the table, Gail picked up the saltshaker and stared at it. Maybe she should hide it. Jacob was so unused to getting his own food that if she put it in one of the kitchen cupboards, she could be sure he would never find it. There were certainly other things hidden away in the house that he had never found. She couldn't be sure what he would do if he did find them: lecture her on wasteful spending, laugh at her silly shopping habit, or maybe even take pride because he made enough money to keep his wife in such style. She wasn't sure which she was more afraid of—which would make her feel worse.

She shook her head a little to clear away thoughts she didn't want to have and focused on fitting the dishes into the dishwasher in the order she preferred. She set it to eco wash and wiped her hands off on a dishcloth, took a last look around the kitchen to be sure everything was just where it should be, and then turned off the lights.

Walking into the den, she sat in the armchair across from her husband's. He was staring moodily at the TV, one hand absently stroking Riley's fur. Gail knew better than to try to make conversation. A rerun of *Law & Order* was on, and it was coming up to Jacob's favorite part of every episode: the courtroom scene. He liked it because he could yell at the screen for getting details wrong, and he could make his own pronouncements on what his arguments would be if this were his case. Gail did not understand how this brought him such pleasure (surely working as a lawyer all day made him long for a break?), but since it did, she said nothing about it. He seemed to get so little pleasure from anything lately.

When was the last time she herself had felt true happiness? Gail searched her memory. Nicole and Aaron's wedding, maybe—a blessed day when everyone was still friends and happy. And then everything had gone wrong. Jacob seemed to lose his mind, deciding his longtime friend and business partner was someone he could no longer trust, someone he had to oppose in every way, torpedoing Michael's bid for judgeship and stealing clients when Jacob struck out on his own. Gail begged Jacob to explain what had happened. She was sure that something very serious must have happened for Jacob to take such drastic action and tear apart not just his partnership but the friendship between two families, not to mention sending shock waves through Nicole and Aaron's new marriage. Surely Michael must have done something to deserve this. Surely Jacob, who had for years been acting more and more selfishly, still needed a reason to act in such a way.

It was a painful day when Gail realized that there was no reason for Jacob's greed and selfishness. He had just grown too big, and it made him act monstrously.

The day she realized that, Gail bought five Chanel dresses and shoes to match. She felt sick when she realized Jacob had become someone so different from the man she had fallen in love with, and after her spending spree, she felt even sicker. She was using what felt like dirty money to try to make herself feel better. So, the clothes hung in their fancy garment bags, and the shoes sat nestled in their tissue paper, making her feel guilty whenever she thought about them.

Jerry Orbach's eyebrows jumped up and down on the TV screen, and Jacob started to yell in rhythm with the actor's gesticulations. *It must be a rerun, then.* Had Jacob yelled the same suggestions at the screen when it was first on, or were these new ideas, wisdom gleaned from his additional years of work? Gail ran her right thumb over her engagement ring in a quick couple of circles, almost as if she were summoning a genie. It was a tic she had developed over the years, and most of the time, she was unaware she was doing it. But tonight, she caught herself, and she stared down at the large diamond in its gold band.

When Jacob had presented it to her those many years ago, she had been overwhelmed at the size of the diamond and the thought that he really wanted her, that this was happening. It wasn't until after the wedding that she wondered if she should have told him the ring wasn't to her taste, but by then it seemed too late. She found that, over time, it grew on her, and now when she looked at it, she saw its bulkiness as charming, rather like the tall, gruff man who had given it to her.

That was the main thing, wasn't it? To find the diamond in the rough, the good in the bad. She had agreed to forever, in sickness and in health, for better and for worse. This might be a darker period in their marriage, but Gail had made a promise, and she was a woman who kept her promises.

Law & Order's credits started to roll. Jacob placed Riley on the floor and used the remote to turn the TV off.

"I'm headed to bed," he said. "Guess I should get a good night's rest before I have to go to my playdate tomorrow."

"That's a good idea," Gail replied, biting her tongue to keep from telling him to stop sulking like a child. He looked tired, and the news from Dr. Lowy had not been good; she did want him to get some sleep. Maybe he would perk up in the morning. She hoped so because tomorrow was going to be an even bigger deal than he knew.

CHAPTER SEVEN

The next day, Jacob obediently drove over to his daughter's house to watch the game with his son-in-law. He couldn't admit it out loud, but he did feel bad about the way he treated Aaron. After all, Aaron and Nicole had grown up together. Jacob had many fond memories of Aaron as a kid—tossing a baseball with him and Michael in the yard on a hot day while the girls watched from the shade, talking with him after his SAT results about whether he wanted to follow his father into the law; and later, watching his shy steps to ask Nicole out, embracing him after the wedding ceremony. He missed Aaron when he thought about it. It wasn't Aaron's fault that Jacob and Michael weren't talking. If Jacob really thought about it, he knew it was his fault alone that he and Michael weren't talking. But he didn't want to think about either of those things. So he didn't.

He struggled getting up the walkway to Nicole's front door, and he took a second to get his breathing back to normal before ringing the bell. Nicole answered the door almost immediately, her blond hair curving around her head in a sleek bob, her pretty features accentuated by light makeup. His lovely daughter. Jacob usually thought in terms of what he earned and what he deserved, but with Nicole, he just knew he was lucky.

"Hi, Dad. How are you feeling?" Nicole said.

"I'm fine. Ready to watch the Lakers redeem themselves. Where's that husband of yours?"

"Aaron, Dad."

"Yes, I know his name is Aaron, thank you," Jacob retorted. "Where is he? Are you going to invite me in?"

"Sorry, Dad, Aaron had to run out. I was just going to go put some air in my tires. Want to come with?"

"Do I have a choice?" Jacob grumbled.

"Nope!" Nicole said brightly. Jacob had to laugh a little at that.

Jacob thought her tires looked fine, but he didn't say anything. She was proud of that car, the first one she'd bought new all by herself, and if she wanted to obsess over the tires, he wasn't going to get in her way.

Twenty minutes and four unnecessarily topped-up tires later, they were on the road again, but they didn't head back to Nicole's house. Instead, they seemed to be heading toward the gated community Jacob and Gail called home.

"If you drive any slower, you're going to get a ticket," Jacob remarked.

"Well then, my father can represent me in court," Nicole replied. She slowed to a stop to enter the code at the gate.

"Why are we here?" Jacob asked as they drove past the gate into the shaded streets of his neighborhood.

"You live here."

"I am aware of that, sweetheart. But my car is now at your house," Jacob pointed out.

"Dad. Stop being so uncooperative," Nicole remonstrated.

"Uncooperative? You invite me over to your house, as soon as I get there you tell me I can't come in, I dutifully come with you to the gas station, and now you drive me to my own house. I think I deserve an explanation," Jacob complained.

"It will all make sense very soon," Nicole said, pulling into the driveway and turning the engine off. She opened her purse and pulled out a blindfold. Jacob frowned at it.

"What are you doing?" Jacob asked.

"Dad, stop with the questions. We're not in a courtroom," Nicole said, tying the blindfold around his eyes. Jacob shook his head a little, making it hard for her.

"Does your mother know about this? What a stupid question. Of course, she does." Jacob suddenly realized what day it was, and what was going on. He hadn't asked for this. He didn't like surprises. He didn't like things he couldn't control. They knew that. He reached up to remove the blindfold, but Nicole jabbed him in the chest.

"Hey, that hurt!" Jacob exclaimed.

"Dad, I am warning you," Nicole said, tying the blindfold tighter. "I just need you to be a good boy and step out of the car. And for once in your life, try to please someone else."

"What's that supposed to mean?" Jacob demanded.

"Nothing, Dad," Nicole sighed. "Okay. I am going to get out and walk around the car and open the door. While I do that, you are going to stay in your seat. Is that understood?"

Jacob let out his own sigh and said, "I don't think I have much choice." That seemed to satisfy Nicole, who got out of the car and came around to the passenger side. She grabbed his arm and told him to swing his legs out of the car and step up slowly. It took a couple tries for Jacob to wriggle around and get the right leverage to heave himself out of the seat.

"Remember my wedding?" Nicole said, linking her arm through his.

"How could I forget? I could have a new boat for all the money I spent," Jacob lamented.

"But you wouldn't have the memories. Anyway, remember how we walked down the aisle? Well, we are about to do it again!" She shut the car door, startling nearby birds, who flew overhead in a noisy flurry.

"Those damn parrots. They're wild," Jacob grumbled. "They circle the neighborhood all day long and make a racket. If I had a gun, I would shoot them."

"Oh, now I find out, after twenty-five years, that my dad is Rambo," Nicole joked. "Okay, Dad, walk slowly. And when I tell you, I want to see a big smile." They started walking up the drive to the house.

"This is ridiculous," Jacob vented. "Your mother knows how much I hate surprises!"

"She sure does, Dad. We all know how everything annoys you. But today, do it for us," Nicole commanded. Jacob faltered a little, and Nicole gripped his arm more tightly. *Everything annoys me?* That seemed a bit harsh. And last night, with Gail reminding him of all the things she thought he'd done badly, after Dr. Lowy giving him the third degree about the way he lived. Why was everyone a critic all of a sudden? He was a grown man just trying to live his life the way he wanted. It wasn't like he needed instructions.

They approached the front door of Jacob's massive house, and Nicole slowed them to a stop.

"Are you ready, Dad?" Her grip tightened again, warning him that he had better not try to bolt.

"Do I at least get a final cigarette before facing the firing squad?"

"Dad," Nicole said warningly.

"Fine. Just get this over with."

"Okay. I'm going to open the door. And as I do, I want you to remove the blindfold, and I want to see that big smile. Just like when the Lakers won the championship. Any questions?"

Jacob put his shoulders back and stood straighter, ready for the assault of well-wishers.

"Here we go," Nicole said. "Remove that blindfold!"

Shouts of "Surprise!" and "Happy birthday!" hit Jacob like bullets, and he jerked his head in every direction as if to deflect the sounds from hitting him. He squinted in the sudden light. His daughter prodded him in his side.

"Where's that smile, Dad?"

Jacob plastered a grin on his face. Nicole nodded. "I'm going to let go of your arm now, and you're going to promise me that you will behave." Nicole peered into his face. Jacob managed a nod of assent, and Nicole flashed him a smile before melting into the gathering crowd.

Jacob looked around him and saw a *Happy Birthday* banner stretching across the far window of the living room. Friends, colleagues, and neighbors filled the entryway, ducking under an arch of brightly colored balloons to get close and shake his hand, give him a hug, plant kisses on his cheek. Gail, decked out in a stunning dress and a party-store tiara, squeezed through and held her husband's hand. She looked beautiful.

"Are you mad?" she asked as she placed a crown to match her tiara on his head. "It's your fiftieth birthday and I wanted—"

"It is wonderful. Thank you," Jacob said. He drew her to him and kissed her. "But I think I have earned a drink." Shaking hands and saying, "Yes, I was surprised!" to the well-wishers around him, Jacob made his way through the living room into the backyard. Emotions swirled inside him: pride at how many people were here to celebrate him, annoyance that he wasn't consulted, gratitude to his wife and daughter for putting the effort in, and embarrassment at being surprised.

The caterer greeted him outside. "Happy birthday, Mr. Abrams. What can I get you?"

"How about a gun with one bullet," Jacob suggested.

"But you haven't seen my bill yet!" the caterer joked. "Kidding. What can I get you?"

"If you can direct me to the bar, that'll be a good start," Jacob said. The caterer pointed to the large tree on the side of the lawn, and Jacob walked over quickly before anyone else could greet him and slow his ability to get a drink fast. He'd just made it when Rabbi Eisel walked up.

"Scotch, straight up," Jacob said to the bartender. Turning to the older gentleman at his side, he asked, "And what can I get you, Rabbi?"

"I am fine, thank you," Rabbi Eisel said, gesturing to the glass of soda water in his hand. Jacob took the scotch in one shot and motioned for a second.

"You know, Jacob, you are very blessed," the rabbi said. "A beautiful wife who loves you. Wonderful family. God is watching over you."

"Thank you, Rabbi. But it's also a lot of hard work. I am a self-made man. No one helped me," Jacob said, patting the rabbi on the back and heading off to get some food. He didn't need a lecture on gratitude on his damn birthday, of all days. He was smiling, he'd said thank you to Gail—what else did people want from him?

He was halfway through a plate of pasta when Dr. Lowy approached him.

"Gail went all out," George remarked.

"Yeah, she did. And this is pasta! Not that crap she cooked last night, thanks to you," Jacob said accusingly through a mouthful of creamy sauce.

"She's only watching out for you," George said. "And I don't recall pasta Alfredo being on the diet I prescribed." Jacob inhaled another forkful.

"Oh, I guarantee that it is not," Jacob said. George shook his head ruefully, then smiled.

"By the way, thanks for the Laker seats." Seeing Jacob's puzzled look, he said, "Oh you don't know. Well, you'll find out." He patted Jacob on the shoulder and walked toward the bar. Jacob looked around for Gail but saw Nicole and Aaron approaching.

"I see you're smiling, Dad. Good job," Nicole teased. Jacob frowned at her in mock annoyance. "Open our present, Dad." She held out a small box.

"You didn't have to get me anything," Jacob said as he set his plate down and reached for the box.

"We hope you like it," Nicole said. Aaron didn't say anything, Jacob noticed. Inside the box, Jacob found an official Lakers watch, with a band of Lakers yellow and purple.

"It's a limited edition," Nicole said eagerly.

"Thank you, sweetheart," Jacob said warmly. "Thank you, Aaron." He gave Nicole a kiss and reached out to awkwardly hug Aaron, who didn't hug back. Well, it was understandable.

"Promise you'll wear it," Nicole said.

"I will," Jacob promised.

"To Hawaii?"

"Where?"

CHAPTER EIGHT

Jacob shifted in his chair, muttering. *With the prices you pay to fly nowadays, you'd think they could afford to make their waiting areas more comfortable,* he mentally griped. Gail had already mentioned that the American Airlines lounge armchairs were much better than the hard plastic seats of the regular waiting area and continued to read her magazine. Electronic chimes sounded overhead, indicating yet another airport announcement.

"This is an announcement for those passengers on American Airlines flight 616, nonstop service from Los Angeles to Maui," the airline employee stated. "The flight has been delayed. We should be departing at 5:30, so we will start boarding at 4:50. As soon as we have more information, we will pass it on to you. Again, this announcement is for passengers holding tickets on flight 616."

"So, we rushed to the airport because you're always nervous we are going to miss our flight, and now we're stuck here," Jacob complained.

"Jacob, do you have someplace else to be?" Gail asked, looking up from her magazine. "Why don't you take a walk? I'm going to call Nicole."

"I think I will get a drink first. Want anything?" he offered. Gail shook her head and picked up her purse to search for her phone.

Jacob started the short walk to the lounge bar, cracking his neck as he went. All that walking and standing in line at security and walking some more in the airport had made his knees sore, and he knew it wasn't going to get any better on the long flight ahead. Dr. Lowy and Gail might have opinions about how much he should drink, but he needed at least one in order to cope with this flight.

The bartender was stacking glasses as Jacob approached. He had the kind of olive-skinned complexion and dark hair found in the Mediterranean, and he wore his long hair loose around his shoulders, reminding Jacob of Fabio. He had a cleft chin like Cary Grant. Jacob bet the ladies loved it. The bartender looked sharp in his white shirt and black bow tie, and Jacob was glad he wasn't one of those travelers who wore their pajamas to fly in; he felt better about approaching this man in his tailored casual clothes. Then he wondered why he cared at all what some bartender might think of him and shook his head to clear away the thought.

"Scotch, straight up," he ordered.

"You got it," the bartender said amiably. Jacob noticed a bowl of nuts and pounced, shoving a large handful into his mouth as he looked up at the TV behind the bar. It was tuned to a golf match.

"Would you mind if we changed channels?" he asked. The bartender handed him the remote and the shot of scotch. Jacob navigated to ESPN and threw back the drink.

"You a Lakers fan?" he asked, the tingle of scotch in his throat loosening him up slightly and making him feel almost friendly.

"No," the bartender replied.

"Not from around here?"

"Spent a little bit of time everywhere. Wherever I am needed."

And with that slightly mysterious statement, the bartender turned his back and resumed stacking glasses from the dishwasher. Jacob shoved more nuts in his mouth while watching the game. Then, with only three seconds left on the clock, Kobe made an amazing three-pointer.

"Yes! Nice shot!" Jacob whooped. "We need to celebrate. Bartender."

"Yeah?" he said, turning.

"Another round."

After pouring the second drink down his throat and scrabbling around for another handful of nuts from the now nearly empty bowl, Jacob appraised the bartender and spoke again.

"You probably get a lot of action, huh?"

"Excuse me?" the bartender said, glancing up.

"You know. You're a good-looking guy." The bartender didn't respond. Jacob continued, "But guys like me have to work a little harder. And I am a self-made man."

The bartender cleared away the bowl of nuts and began to wipe up the mess of crumbs Jacob had made.

"You see that woman over there? The redhead. Nice rack, huh?" Jacob carried on. "No ring on her finger. And I bet she is wild. If I got her on my boat, after a few drinks she would be down on her knees before I even left the harbor."

"Anything else I can get you, sir?" the bartender asked, his face neutral. *No fun, this guy*, Jacob thought.

"Yeah, get the plane off the ground?" he joked, still in a good mood from the Lakers' win and his two shots of scotch.

"Well, I can't help you there. But I am sure you will be on your way shortly," the bartender replied. Then he offered his hand to Jacob and said, "Perhaps we will meet again?"

Jacob took the bartender's hand to shake. But when he tried to release the grip, he felt a tightness in his chest. It was like nothing he had ever experienced before. His whole body seemed to tighten around the center of his chest. He took a deep breath, then coughed and started to say that maybe he wasn't feeling so well. Suddenly, the bartender released his hand, and the tightness immediately dissipated.

Dazed, Jacob goggled at the bartender, but the man's face was inscrutable, his eyes somehow in shadow. Jacob walked away, massaging his chest. He dropped his hand quickly when he passed the redhead and flashed her a smile. A little heartburn wasn't going to get in his way. *And that's all it was, surely.*

"American Airlines flight 616, nonstop service to Maui, boarding has begun," the voice overhead droned. Jacob held out his hand to Gail and helped her to her feet.

"Everything all right?" Gail asked.

"Yeah, of course," Jacob said. "Let's go."

He was already planning to order another scotch as soon as they were settled in their seats. It might have only been heartburn, but he still felt a little off balance, almost like he'd missed something important.

CHAPTER NINE

Gail watched Jacob walk away toward the American Airlines lounge bar as she held the phone to her ear, listening to it ring. "Hi, this is Nicole, but I can't come to the phone right now. Leave a message!" Gail hung up and put her phone back in her purse. She would have left a message just to say hi, but Nicole had confessed that she usually did not listen to her messages and sometimes just deleted them all when they piled up. Gail had been slightly horrified; what if there was something important in there? If it was so important, they would call back, Nicole explained. Apparently, no one listened to their messages nowadays.

A far cry from how it used to be. Even just a few decades ago, it had been a big deal when they got an answering machine and, later, caller ID. Now, no one cared about your call unless you tried over and over. Well, maybe there was something to that. She was trying over and over with Jacob, wasn't she? Was that not what this whole birthday party and trip to Hawaii was about? Trying to recapture the spark in her marriage, trying to prove to herself that she was the good wife everyone thought she was?

Not to say she was unfaithful—of course not. She kept her promises, after all. But she had been so unhappy in the past few years with Jacob that she felt almost unfaithful in her heart. He was dreadfully negative all the time, and where she used to see his caustic wit as a sign of intelligence, now she just found it mean and tiring. Then there was this whole business with Ms. Harris, a client of Jacob's who might be more than a client. Jacob swore she was not, that nothing had happened between them, but Gail saw his attraction to her, and she couldn't be sure he had not acted on that attraction. That was a terrible thing, to not be able to trust her husband of nearly thirty years. This was why she felt like a bad wife. She should be able to trust him; she should be better at supporting him the way she had when they were first married.

She thought back to their first place, an apartment in an okay but not great neighborhood, with one bedroom, a hideous peach-colored bathroom, and just enough room in the living room for a couch and a TV. It was not what Jacob wanted, but he knew they would not be there long. Gail, who had come from a comfortable background, loved the dingy little apartment. It was theirs, and that was what mattered. She threw herself into homemaking, trying out new recipes, sewing curtains for the kitchen, even taking up a little knitting. She had always been a decent cook, and now that she was no longer working as a secretary, she had the time to really improve her skills, and she became a great one. The sewing and knitting, however, were not to her taste, and she gave those up after the first set of badly hemmed curtains and a comically oversized knit cap.

Back then, Jacob was working at the district attorney's office, putting in the long hours of a new lawyer who needed to prove himself to his superiors. Gail had the whole day to herself, and she paged through magazines, taking the quizzes, casting a critical eye over the clothes, and picking out the ones she would buy when Jacob made partner at a firm sometime in the future. She picked out recipes and spent hours buying the ingredients from different stores—the deli on this corner, the imported Italian oils shop down this street—and assembling them into delicious meals. Jacob would come home around seven, ravenous for dinner and, after, for her. They would leave the dishes in the sink and go to the bedroom, making love and laughing, making plans for the future that would surely be as wonderful as this present. In the mornings, Jacob would shower for work while she fixed him a quick breakfast, and then he would be gone. She would do the dishes from the night before, and as they dried in the rack next to the sink, she would open up a magazine and start it all over again.

After a couple years, they had Nicole, and they moved to a small starter home. That was a difficult time. The move meant that Jacob had a longer commute to work, and of course taking care of a newborn was exhausting. Now, instead of lazy mornings paging through magazines, Gail was stuck in an endless cycle of feeding, changing, and soothing. The elaborate meals came to a stop, and she barely had time to throw together spaghetti with sauce from a jar. Sweet Jacob did not complain. He could see that his wife was working hard, just as he was working hard to provide for her and for their precious baby girl. So even though she felt she didn't sleep for two years, and Jacob was home even less often than before, Gail still thought of those difficult early years as good ones. They were working together to make a good life for themselves and for Nicole.

Things changed when Jacob went to work with Michael and Mr. Greenbaum. They were able to afford a bigger house, in a neighborhood with good schools. Nicole and Diane got along right away, and Gail was grateful to have a friend to talk with about raising a baby, running a household, and living with a lawyer in a demanding job. It was such a comfort to have someone who understood all the challenges Gail was facing.

Well, not all of them. Gail loved Jacob very much and would not switch him for anyone, but he never did get less gruff, and in fact he got more boastful the more successful he was, unlike Michael, who was a gentle soul for whom boasting was a foreign idea. Diane wouldn't know what it was like to be the wife of someone who talked about how much money he had made off a recent case, how mortifying it was for Gail to be at a cocktail party with him and hear him taunt junior members of the legal team who were not making as much as he had at their age. Was Gail a little jealous of her?

Gail didn't know what to do about it. Before she and Jacob had married, her mother told her that she would have to work hard to get the good out of her marriage. Jacob had good in him, but he kept it buried under layers of an unhealthy ego. That ego had been part of what attracted her to him—the confidence he carried. And it seemed to affect everyone he met, including shy Gail, who had not had many boyfriends and was worried she was too mousy for men to pay attention to. When Jacob turned his attention to her, all his confidence in himself and what he would accomplish shining off of him somehow warmed her, and she felt herself open up like a flower in the sun.

She had been raised by quite traditional parents and had a lot of ideas about what a wife owed a husband anyway, and in addition she felt grateful to Jacob for recognizing in her something worth picking out of the crowd, for showing her that she was sexy and interesting and worthy of his attention. She wanted to support him as much for that as for the fact that she was his wife.

So his arrogance continued to get a pass as he grew more successful with Michael and Mr. Greenbaum. Now that she had everything she wanted—now that they were settled in a good home, raising a child together, building the future they had talked about so often with such excitement—she would be crazy to complain about the behavior of the man who made it all possible. Gail resolved to be more forgiving, more generous. If he maybe sounded a little mean in some of his comments, he didn't mean anything by it. That was just Jacob.

This was the decision Gail had made nearly twenty-five years ago, and she had kept to that attitude for nearly the whole time since. He continued to provide, their standard of living continued to improve, and they raised a beautiful and accomplished daughter. Gail continued to have everything she wanted. She could let the more uncouth and unkind remarks slip by, with only a few chastening words here and there.

Then he betrayed Michael and turned all their lives upside down. Without even realizing she was doing it, Gail started scolding Jacob every time he said something thoughtless. She brought up charity events and pressed him to speak kindly of others. Sitting in the airport lounge, her thumb rubbing her engagement ring, Gail saw that she had made a decision two and a half years ago, a decision to stand up for herself more, and for others. Was this being a bad wife? She had been thinking of it that way, thinking of herself as unsupportive. But now she wondered if maybe what she was doing was actually the supportive thing to do—encouraging her husband to be the best version of himself.

She looked over at the bar and saw Jacob, talking to the bartender, gesture to his right. She followed his pointed finger and saw a busty woman in red, scrolling through something on her phone. Gail sighed. This was another way Jacob needed to improve and become a better version of himself. Apparently, Ms. Harris was not enough, and he needed to check out other women even while on vacation with his wife, who not for nothing had had an expensive haircut and mani-pedi before they left, and who was wearing a brand-new outfit that showed off her trim figure, none of which had received so much as a comment from Jacob. Would he notice or care about the swimsuit she had packed? She had given up bikinis several years ago, but she could still pull off a stylish swimsuit with a daringly low back. She sighed. She would have to wait and see. She was trying over and over, right? Here was another new start.

CHAPTER TEN

Nicole looked at the weather for Hawaii on her phone. *Eighty-three degrees—not bad.* She hoped her parents were having a good time. Jacob had looked shocked when she mentioned Hawaii, and she was still annoyed that Gail hadn't warned him; Nicole was left with the task of explaining to her dad that he was going to Hawaii for a week as a birthday treat. He was happy enough about it, although a little annoyed that he'd had so little warning to get things sorted at work before heading out. Of course, his assistant Donna had been in on it, so she'd done a lot of the work behind the scenes already.

Nicole often felt like she was the one doing the behind-the-scenes work, in the family. She didn't know when it had started, exactly. Certainly as a child she'd felt like both her parents were equally involved in her life, but as she grew into adolescence, it seemed like her father was working more and more, and she only saw him on weekends and special occasions. Her mother, who used to insist on family dinners every night, didn't object after a while when they became less regular. Gail used to joke about the bored rich housewives in their neighborhood, but over the years, as she grew accustomed to the comforts of wealth, she didn't joke about them as much. She used to challenge Jacob on his more outrageous statements about charity and the poor, but after a while she did it more resignedly, as if this was the price she paid for her lifestyle.

Nicole, the observant only child, noticed this in her teens and increasingly felt like she was the bridge between her parents, the only thing they could still agree on. What they agreed on was that Nicole needed to be the best and have the best, and while Nicole still had the attitude that she needed to work for the good things in life, she started to resent the pressure she felt from them. She felt like she had to be the perfect child in order to keep their family working, or her parents wouldn't even talk to each other anymore.

Now, as a grown woman who'd achieved all the things her parents expected of her, she felt that pressure less. And in recent years, her mother seemed to come around to the idea of pushing back more on Jacob's mean-spirited talk so Nicole didn't have to do it herself or just watch it happen with no protest.

But as Nicole put her phone down and turned back to her computer to continue with the report she'd been working on all morning, she was hit with a wave of sadness. She had not achieved *all* the things her parents expected of her. There was one big, gaping hole in her life and in her parents' lives. Not that her dad ever mentioned it to her, and her mom tried to be sensitive, but Nicole couldn't pretend that "When are you giving us a grandchild?" hadn't been said, and more than once.

Nicole wanted a child, desperately. She had married a little younger than her friends, but now they were all getting married and planning to start their families right away. Where once she had felt like she was ahead of things, she now felt behind. She saw babies everywhere—smiling up from strollers in the park, waving at her from car seats on the highway, throwing food onto the ground from their high chairs in restaurants. Even when she saw a baby having a screaming fit in the grocery store, she felt a pang of longing.

She was positive she could keep her career and have the baby. Her mother wasn't so sure, but it was a different time now. No, that wasn't the issue. The issue was that her husband really knew how to hold a grudge.

Ever since her father had suddenly gone crazy and refused to back Aaron's father's bid for a judgeship, not long after Nicole and Aaron had married, Aaron refused to say Jacob's name. Sometimes he would call him "JJ," as in Jacob the Jerk, but he wouldn't talk about him, and he didn't want to listen to Nicole mention him either. He'd agreed to go to Jacob's fiftieth birthday after weeks of begging on Nicole's part, and the look of fury on his face when Jacob awkwardly hugged him for the Lakers watch was quite a sight.

It was so unfair. Nicole and Aaron had grown up together, as their fathers had been business partners their entire lives. They got married when things were good, and Nicole had expected a future as bright as the past had been. She and Aaron even had one or two conversations about when they should start trying to get pregnant. And then her father had started a feud for no good reason that she could see, and he didn't seem to notice or care that it affected everyone else's lives.

Aaron was so enraged by Jacob's treatment of Michael that he refused to consider giving Jacob a grandchild. The couple of times Nicole had found the courage to bring it up, Aaron said that Jacob didn't deserve the joy of a grandchild. Nicole tried to reason with him, saying that Aaron couldn't punish everyone just to spite her father. And Aaron had once admitted that he knew it was irrational, and that the grudge couldn't last forever, but for now he just could not consider conceiving a child.

So, Nicole was stuck, loving her husband and loving her father, unable to talk about either of them with the other. She wanted a baby more than just about anything. Sometimes she was overwhelmed with the unfairness of it all.

CHAPTER ELEVEN

The tropical breeze felt good on Jacob's skin after the stale air of the plane. As he and Gail gathered their bags and he paid the taxi driver, he felt back to his normal self. A couple scotches on the plane, and only one argument with Gail about how much he was drinking and how much salt he was adding to his meal, meant he was in a pretty good place. He looked approvingly at the doorless lobby, lush with ferns and exotic flowers. *These would look good in my office lobby*, he thought. Which reminded him that he should check his messages.

A pretty young woman approached Jacob and Gail with colorful leis in her hands. "Aloha," she said as she placed a lei over Gail's head.

"Why, thank you!" Gail said, smiling.

"Aloha," the hotel employee said, attempting to put the second lei over Jacob's head. But he was already digging in his pocket for his phone and swatted her away. He didn't even glance at the greeter's shocked face.

"I don't need a necklace," he said, "just tell me the Wi-Fi code."

The greeter recovered her welcoming smile and said, "Certainly, sir. The Wi-Fi name is Guest, and the password is, you guessed it, Aloha!" Gail chuckled and the greeter smiled gratefully. Jacob typed in the password and ignored them both.

"I will get the bellboy to bring your bags up to your room," the greeter said. "In the meantime, if you would like to step over to the desk, my colleague would be happy to check you in."

Jacob nodded absently and shuffled over to the desk without even looking up from his phone. He didn't notice how long it took Gail to catch up.

"Aloha, Mr. and Mrs. Abrams. I hope you had a very pleasant journey," the desk clerk said with a smile. Jacob immediately disliked him, with his slicked-back hair and ingratiating smile.

"We did, thank you," Gail said. Jacob continued scrolling through his messages.

"Let's see, we have you here for five nights, an ocean-view suite in our Malakai Tower on the sixth floor. Room 616. Your rate includes our full breakfast. Is that correct?" the oily clerk said.

"Yes," Gail affirmed. Jacob flashed an insincere smile, nose still to his phone.

"Great," the clerk said. "Just sign here. And if I can see your credit card?" Jacob tossed his card on the desk and kept scrolling. Gail took the two room cards the clerk handed her. "Are we celebrating any special occasion?"

"Yes, it's my husband's fiftieth birthday," Gail said with a smile. Jacob nodded without lifting his gaze. This chatter was all fine, but it was taking a long time for his messages to load, and he was getting annoyed.

"Well, happy birthday! I don't know if you have made any reservations, but I highly recommend dining with us in our Haleakala restaurant. In fact, if you would like, I can see if we can reserve a table outdoors for this evening," the clerk offered. "You can sink your feet into the sand while you enjoy the moonlight. It is very romantic."

"That sounds wonderful," Gail enthused. "Jacob?"

"You have really bad reception here," Jacob said, looking up for the first time. "We are spending a lot of money and I expect better!"

"I am so sorry about that," the clerk said. "Perhaps after you get settled you can call me, and I would be happy to make any reservations you would like."

"Fine. And see what you can do about this Wi-Fi. This is the twenty-first century, you know," Jacob said, turning away from the desk and stumping toward the elevators. Gail smiled apologetically at the clerk and followed her husband.

"You were so rude," she said through clenched teeth as they waited for the elevator.

"Screw him, the little weasel," Jacob said contemptuously. "He's the kind of guy I like to chew up in court." They got in the elevator, and Jacob stabbed the button for floor six.

"You embarrass me," Gail said, her mouth still in a tight line.

"What?" Jacob asked.

"What did that man ever do to you? Or the woman with the leis? They're just doing their jobs," Gail said.

"That's just it. They did nothing. But I have done it all by myself," Jacob retorted. How could she be defending some lowly hotel employees against him, a prominent LA lawyer?

The elevator doors opened on the sixth floor and Gail stepped out quickly.

"What does that even mean, all by yourself? No one does anything by themselves, Jacob. We all have help from somewhere," Gail fumed. "Well, you can help yourself all by yourself this afternoon, because I am going shopping. Go fuck yourself!"

Jacob grabbed her hand and tried to leave the elevator with her. Gail shook him off.

"Let go of me."

"I'm sorry," Jacob said. The elevator dinged a warning as the doors stayed open, Jacob half in and half out.

"Do you know how many times in our marriage you've said you're sorry?" Gail asked, sudden exhaustion evident on her face. "And I always forgive you."

"I don't want to fight. What can I do?" Jacob pleaded.

"You can start by going down to the lobby and apologizing to the clerk for your behavior—and that poor girl who tried to give you a lei. It's a sign of hospitality, for crying out loud," Gail said. She nudged him back into the elevator.

"Of course, I'll do that," Jacob said.

As the doors began to close, she said, "And tell the clerk that we would like to dine at seven."

CHAPTER TWELVE

The elevator doors closed on her husband, and Gail stared at them, clutching her purse and taking a deep breath to calm herself. Gail never swore—never. Once, when she was preparing dinner, she had not been paying enough attention to what she was doing and had cut herself quite deeply with the chopping knife. Even then, she only shrieked, "Sugar! That hurts." So she was surprised at herself for using the f-word with Jacob. It just flew out of her mouth, her rage so explosive that she could not help herself. The look on his face was enough to show that he knew what a big deal it was for her to use that kind of language, and some of her anger dissipated as soon as she saw that expression.

As she inserted the key into the lock and opened the door, Gail thought back on the last half hour. She had been all too aware of what was going on out in the lobby. It was a very familiar situation: out in public, Jacob acting like some kind of royalty who didn't need to treat people with basic respect, and Gail left to hold together the fabric of social niceties all by herself. As soon as Jacob pushed aside the greeter trying to give him a lei, Gail felt dismayed. He had been so jovial on the plane, with the drinks at the airport lounge and the scotch with his airplane meal. He even made some jokes with the flight attendants. She had started to relax and think that maybe this vacation would be different from all the other ones, where Jacob brought his courtroom fight mode to everyday interactions.

He had not even noticed that she wasn't with him when he left the greeter and turned toward the check-in desk. Gail had wheeled their bags close together so they would be easy for the bellboy to handle.

"It was a difficult flight for him," she had said apologetically to the greeter.

"Oh, it's fine," the greeter replied. "We just want to make our guests comfortable."

"Thank you, I am sure we will be. It's a beautiful hotel," Gail said. The greeter had nodded and then excused herself to fetch the bellboy. Gail walked quickly over to the check-in desk, hoping to head off whatever rudeness her husband was going to inflict next on the poor hotel staff.

The desk clerk was young, even younger than Nicole. He looked nervous, and Gail wanted to reassure him that he had done nothing wrong. He kept smiling throughout the interaction, although it wavered when Jacob finally bothered to look up from his phone only to yell at the clerk about something that, as far as Gail could tell, should not matter at all, since they were on vacation and should not be checking their emails or phone messages. She had only brought her phone to keep in touch with Nicole. Why would Jacob need to do anything work related while in Hawaii? Gail had carefully arranged things with Donna so that he would not be bothered with client calls or any kind of scheduling issues for ongoing cases. Did he really think he was so important that everything would fall apart without him there for one week?

These were thoughts going through Gail's head while she tried to soothe the desk clerk and get out of there as quickly as possible. The greeter, the desk clerk, the phone—all of it was too much. All of it was Jacob at his most unbearable, and here was Gail, thinking she should try over and over, because marriage was worth it, and their marriage in particular was worth it. He seemed to be proving her wrong, and she was furious with him. Had she made a big mistake?

When he apologized and said he did not want to fight, Gail deflated. He had apologized so many times over the course of their marriage, and she always accepted his apologies. He seemed to mean them when he said them, and she wanted to take him at his word. She wanted his word to mean something. This time, she felt she had to point out to him that this was a pattern. Was it possible he didn't know? Perhaps. Well, now she had said something, and it was up to him to reflect on that in his own time.

Gail looked at the suitcases lined up next to the door and decided she could not face unpacking them right now. She would go shopping, as she had told Jacob she would. She visited the bathroom and retouched her lipstick. Her anger had not brought tears to her eyes, so her mascara was still in place. She stared at herself in the mirror and thought, *Don't go overboard down there, Gail. Don't let yourself go.* She put a stray hair back in place, picked up her purse, and switched off the light.

Downstairs, she found the hotel store easily. As soon as she crossed the threshold, some of the tension left her shoulders. Even though she had never been here before, everything was instantly familiar to her: the music playing at a low volume, the flattering lighting, and the racks of clothes with only a few elegant items each on them. No loud pop music or fluorescent lighting here, no crowds of people flinging clothes all over the place as they searched for the best deal; this was a high-end store, and everything about it reassured Gail.

She walked in the door, and one of the well-dressed women

behind the counter immediately smiled and approached to ask if she needed any assistance.

"I'm just going to take a look around for now," Gail said, and the salesperson smiled and reiterated that she was available as soon as Gail needed her.

Gail was an organized person. She wrote grocery lists and didn't deviate from them. She kept a calendar for both herself and Jacob. Generally, everything had an order and she followed it. But when it came to shopping, she let all of that go. She let herself be led by her impulses, walking to one rack to touch a dress that looked like it had an interesting texture, then drifting to another, distracted by a color she liked. A pair of slacks caught her eye, and she held them up to the light to get a better look. The salesperson materialized at her side.

"We also have that in a lovely peach color, although the lilac is my favorite," the woman said, her low voice fitting in seamlessly with the soothing environment of the store.

"Yes, if I could set this aside, please," Gail said. The salesperson took it away, and Gail continued wandering the store.

She was pleased to find that she wasn't picking up item after item. That had happened before, when she was really upset (witness the Chanels and shoes from when she realized Jacob had blown up their lives for his own greed). She had sometimes shopped in a frenzy, calm on the outside but shaking with anger on the inside and buying as many nice things as she could to attempt to calm that anger, to make her feel in control again.

But today, she was being selective. Maybe that quick pep talk she had given herself in the mirror upstairs had worked. Maybe it was the tropical air or the fact she was on vacation. Whatever the reason, she knew that she was going to buy a few things but not undertake an entire spree. She would maintain control. Her husband might fly off the handle or overeat and drink too much, but Gail could contain herself. Those other times were just aberrations—when she had bought so much that she could scarcely believe the credit cards could cover the expense. Never mind that she had said the same thing to herself before and then had more shopping sprees again. This time would be different.

Ending her reverie with a little toss of her head, Gail replaced the blouse she had been staring at and moved on to the accessories section. She had a vague idea of getting a sort of classic Hawaiian print, not like those loud shirts men wore but something that would remind her she'd been to the tropics after she returned to Los Angeles. One of the scarves seemed to fit the bill, with large, bright flowers on it. The shop girl was again at her side, and Gail gave her the scarf with an appreciative smile. She was certainly earning her commission.

Just as she thought maybe she would take the slacks and the scarf and call it a day, Gail noticed the jewelry counter. She glanced at the rings and bracelets briefly, but she was more interested in the necklaces. Jacob was apologizing to the greeter and desk clerk right now, but if he was really sorry, he would want to show it in diamonds, right?

CHAPTER THIRTEEN

That evening, anyone who saw them in the outdoor section of the restaurant would never have guessed that Jacob and Gail had had a big fight earlier in the day. They sat gazing into each other's eyes in prime seats with an unobstructed view of the waves lapping on the shore. The moonlight shone gently down, the flames of the tiki torches flickered along the perimeter of the restaurant, and the breeze ruffled Gail's hair. The bottle of red wine between them was half drunk, and Gail showed off her new necklace to her husband while a ukulele strummed in the background.

"Thank you for the necklace. Isn't it beautiful?" Gail said, holding the gold chain out so he could admire the heart-shaped diamond hanging from it.

"It certainly is. I'm sure it wasn't on sale," he said, smiling.

"Definitely not!" Gail confirmed, with a smile of her own. The smile faded as she added, "I hope you were sincere in your apology to the hotel clerk and the greeter."

"Of course I was," Jacob reassured her. It hadn't been easy, swallowing his pride and asking the forgiveness of some oily little pip-squeak or the girl who he didn't even remember, but he had promised Gail, and whatever else she might think of him, he was a man of his word. Or at least he wanted to be.

Their server approached the table.

"I just checked, and your sharing courses will be right up," she said. "In the meantime, is there anything I can get you?"

"We're fine, thank you," Jacob said. As she walked away, Gail gave her backside an approving look.

"She is very pretty," Gail commented.

"I wasn't looking," Jacob said.

"You are such a liar. And you can add lying to your ever-growing list of sins," Gail said.

"I added that one a long time ago," Jacob laughed. Catching his wife's look, he cut his laughter short. Not the time for jokes. He reached over and took Gail's hand in his own. "She is very pretty. But I have the most beautiful woman in the world sitting right in front of me."

Gail smiled and squeezed his hand.

"I am sorry for earlier," Jacob said.

"You're forgiven," Gail said. "But you need to be more grateful for what you have." Jacob nodded compliantly. It wasn't the most unreasonable request. People didn't seem to appreciate just how much he had done on his own, but it was true that he had a lot. He could afford to be grateful.

Just then, their server returned with the first sharing course.

"You know," Jacob said mischievously as their server left them alone, "they say that oysters are an aphrodisiac."

"Well, I guess we'll find out if that's true," Gail replied with a flutter of her eyelashes. Jacob grinned. They dug in.

CHAPTER FOURTEEN

Nicole realized she wasn't going to get more work done now. Time to take a late lunch. She gathered up her purse and her cardigan and started for the office door, scrolling through her contact list on her phone until she found her mother's number.

"Mom, hi, it's me," she said as she walked out into the bright Los Angeles air.

"Hi, sweetie," Gail replied. "What are you up to?"

"Taking my lunch. I thought I'd walk up to that new salad fast food place a couple blocks away."

"Walk? In LA?" They both laughed.

"I'm sorry to bother you on your vacation," Nicole said. "I didn't even really think of it; I just called you like normal."

"Oh, that's okay, sweetie," Gail said. "I'm sitting by the pool, just getting some sun before I get ready for lunch."

"Is Dad there?" Nicole asked.

"No, he's in the room," Gail replied, with a slight edge in her voice. *Uh-oh*, Nicole thought, *here it comes.*

"He was so rude to the greeter and the desk clerk," Gail said. There it was. "He was on his phone the whole time we were checking in, and he kept yelling about Wi-Fi. As if we came to Hawaii to be on Wi-Fi! What does he need to check his messages for, anyway? He's on vacation!"

"Well, I guess he's still getting used to the idea, since it was a surprise vacation," Nicole said cautiously.

"Maybe." Gail sounded dubious. "But can't a wife surprise her husband with something nice and not have it be tainted immediately?"

"I don't know, Mom. I'm sure it will be okay in a couple days."

"Oh, probably. I am sure I'm just tired from the plane ride. It's a good thing we live on the coast. It was already a long enough ride for me. Imagine if we lived in New York!"

"Yes, much better to be close to paradise."

"Oh you," Gail said. "Anyway, I shouldn't still be angry about last night. After he apologized to the staff, your father took me to dinner at the restaurant here at the hotel. It was great! We had our toes in the sand while we ate."

"That sounds great, Mom. I'm so glad you're having a nice time."

"I really am. I think I needed this vacation as much as your father did," Gail confessed. "Look, honey, I'm sorry, but if I'm going to be ready for lunch, I've really got to go. Was there anything you wanted to talk about?"

"No, that's okay; don't worry about it, Mom. Have a nice meal."

"Thanks, sweetie. You have a good day. Say hi to Aaron for me."

"I will. Bye, Mom."

"Bye!"

As Nicole put her phone back in her purse, she sighed. That hadn't exactly been the nice conversation she'd been hoping for. Instead, more for her to smooth over. Sometimes she thought she should have followed her father into the law. She certainly had the requisite negotiating skills.

It was funny—she'd been shy as a child, and now no one would describe her as shy. She was outgoing and confident. At her dad's surprise party, she surprised herself with how steely she'd been, getting him out of the car and up to the house without him making a run for it and only minimal fuss. Her mother had given her the task without a second thought, but Nicole had fretted about how best to do it for days. Nicole was a bit of a worrier, no question.

But Gail had been right. Jacob was disinclined to upset his beloved only daughter, and Nicole had a way with him. She seemed to be able to sweet-talk him into things Gail could never browbeat him into, like going meekly into his own surprise party or, once, taking them on a ski vacation to Vail like Gail wanted, rather than the Saint Lucia cruise he'd thought they should do.

Sometimes she worried that she had learned the lessons her father taught a little too well. She caught herself getting quite aggressive in meetings at work, and she didn't like the way she sounded. But then, it was complicated. Sheryl Sandberg reminded her she needed to lean in, and hedge funds were a competitive, high-pressure area of finance, so she needed a certain level of aggression to be successful. And she liked being successful. But her father's need to be successful made him veer into cruelty sometimes. Maybe that was the difference: she was okay with being aggressive and going for the most she could get every time, but not if it meant she had to be unkind or underhanded. She was pretty sure she was on the right side of that line. But in another twenty years, if she kept going the same way, would she find herself on the other side?

That was another thing she had thought about over the last two years, as her family was split horribly down the middle. She could not imagine doing what her father did to anyone she loved as much as Jacob loved Michael, and yet he had done it. Nicole was young, and she had a hard time imagining what two more decades might do to her mindset. Would she become bitter and mean, like her dad seemed to be becoming? Would she become more distant and resigned, like her mom was? Would she try to avoid all conflict and always be the peacemaker, like Diane?

She hoped she would be like Michael, actually. He seemed to be dealing with it the best out of any of them. He had not forgiven Jacob, just as Aaron hadn't, but he didn't badmouth him to Nicole or make her feel guilty for her father's sins. He kept working, doing a certain amount of pro bono work every year as part of his good works. He donated to charity and took his wife on nice vacations. He appreciated his good fortune and shared it with others. That was the model Nicole was looking for—how to grow into middle age gracefully. If she ever had a child, that was the kind of behavior she would want to model for them.

Great, she thought. *I'm back at babies again. How do I always end up here?*

She left the salad bar and emerged into the LA sunshine. She looked down at her 2.5-inch heels and smiled ruefully; she should have changed into sneakers before making this trip. *Oh well, I'm here now.* She readjusted her shirt over her skirt, smoothed back her hair from her face, and set out for the office. She was Nicole Abrams Green, and she could handle anything. Even an LA walk in heels.

CHAPTER FIFTEEN

A little before dawn, Jacob jerked awake suddenly. He knew right away that it was no good trying to go back to sleep; he was awake now. *Must be the jet lag or something*, he thought. He looked over at Gail, breathing peacefully in the last of the moonlight streaming through their window. He wouldn't bother her. He would go for a walk along the beach. As quietly as he could, he slipped on some shorts, a shirt, and his loafers. He stole out the door and let it close gently behind him.

Walking in sand was harder than Jacob remembered; he wondered when he'd last done so. He was panting with effort by the time he made it down to the shore. He bent over and removed his shoes, letting the water roll over his toes until it no longer felt cold. He picked a direction at random and started walking on the empty beach.

Last night was the first time he and Gail had been intimate in longer than Jacob cared to admit. There was nothing wrong with his equipment, he would be the first to point out to anyone who asked, and although he was a little heavy (*okay, morbidly obese, Dr. Lowy*), that didn't seem to bother Gail too much. But lately, they seemed to be arguing more and more frequently, so she was never in the mood. If he really thought about it, the arguments were mostly about ways he had behaved or things he had done that Gail thought were unkind or thoughtless.

This realization so upset him that he stumbled and lost his balance. Just then, a man appeared by his side, reaching out to assist.

"Do you need help?" the stranger asked.

"Thanks, I must have tripped over that piece of driftwood," Jacob said, grabbing the outstretched hand.

Immediately, Jacob felt an intense pressure in the center of his chest, a tightening just like he'd felt before their flight the day before. Disoriented, he looked up into the sky and saw a small patch of whitish clouds against the lightening sky. He tried to pull back from the stranger's grip, but the pain was too intense. He started sweating, and his vision blurred. Finally, he managed to yank his hand back, and the pain lessened. The small patch of white in the sky disappeared as well. Leaning on his knee to leverage himself to his feet, Jacob got his first good look at the stranger.

"You look familiar," Jacob said. The man's hair was tied back in a ponytail, and he was wearing a Billabong shirt and board shorts, but that cleft chin was unmistakable.

"Well, they say everyone has a double," the stranger replied casually, seemingly unaware of the alarming experience Jacob had just undergone.

"You don't work at the American lounge at LAX, do you?" Jacob asked, peering at him. "I could swear I saw you yesterday."

"Sorry, wasn't me." The stranger shrugged. Jacob took a deep breath and glanced warily at the man.

"That's quite a grip you have," he noted.

"So I have been told," the stranger said. His eyes were shadowed in the dark, and Jacob couldn't see them properly. The stranger's face was impassive, just as the bartender's had been.

"Well, be careful where you walk," the stranger said, reaching out for a handshake, which Jacob deflected by massaging his chest. The stranger walked away into the rising sun. Before Jacob could try to make sense of what had just happened, he heard a noise behind him. He turned and saw a woman sitting on a blanket just a few feet away.

"Have you been sitting here? I didn't see you a minute ago," Jacob said, feeling more disoriented than ever.

"The sunrise can play tricks on your eyes," the woman suggested.

"I guess," Jacob said uncertainly. The woman motioned for him to join her on the blanket, and he was still a little shaky, so he did, still massaging his chest. The woman reached out and lightly touched his shoulder, and suddenly the pain in his chest was completely gone.

Jacob took a closer look at this strange woman whose touch soothed as much as the strange man's touch had hurt. Yes, she was about Gail's age, but that was about all they had in common. She wore no makeup, and unlike his wife's stylish hairstyle, this woman's long gray hair was worn loose and a little messy. She was dressed in gray yoga pants and a pale-pink T-shirt, and she was also barefoot. She noticed him looking at her and smiled.

"My name is Laura," she offered.

"Jacob," he said. "Are you from here?"

"I have lived all over," Laura replied.

"Military family? Moved around a lot?" Jacob inquired.

"Something like that," Laura said noncommittally. A gentle breeze came up, and strands of Laura's long hair floated in the air. "Jacob, you look worried," Laura said. "Are you all right?"

"I am fine," Jacob said in a voice that shook a little.

"You're not convincing me," Laura said, smiling.

Jacob laughed. "That's funny. That's what I do for a living— convince people."

"Oh?"

"Yeah, I'm a criminal attorney," Jacob said, sitting up a bit straighter when he said it.

"I see," Laura said. "And do you find your work rewarding?"

"Well, let me say this," Jacob said. "If my clients pay me enough, it is rewarding." He waited for her to laugh at his little joke, but she just stared at him steadily. Okay, so maybe she didn't have a great sense of humor.

"You ever do something you regret?" she asked.

"No one is perfect," Jacob replied, caught a little off guard. "We have all made mistakes."

"No mistake that you can ever make is greater than God's power to fix it," Laura said firmly. Again, Jacob laughed.

"I haven't spoken to God in a long time. In fact, he's probably forgotten my name."

The sun had risen higher in the sky, and it cast a golden glow over Laura's face as she looked at him sympathetically.

"You would be surprised, Jacob. God is always watching and listening."

Normally, Jacob wouldn't have time for this God stuff, but she said it so simply and with such certainty that Jacob didn't mind. In fact, he found it kind of comforting. He inhaled a deep breath of fresh air and turned to face the rising sun. He felt refreshed. He turned back to Laura to ask her how often she talked to God, but she was gone.

CHAPTER SIXTEEN

Nicole was typing away on her computer, happily "in the zone" in the quiet of an empty office early in the morning, when suddenly she felt a shock. It was as if she'd touched an electrical outlet; the jolt went straight through her, and she sat back in her chair, eyes wide. What was that all about? She cautiously put her right hand on her chest and pressed down over her heart, which was beating a million miles a minute. Quickly, she googled "heart attack symptoms." She stood and walked around her cubicle, swinging her arms and saying her name out loud (she really was grateful the office was empty). Okay, she didn't seem to be having a heart attack. An extreme case of someone walking over her grave and giving her the chills? Maybe.

It had felt ominous, though, like something was wrong—if not with her, then with someone else. She glanced at the clock: 7:15 a.m. She picked up her phone and called Aaron's cell.

"Hello?" Aaron said, sounding a bit winded from his morning treadmill run.

"Aaron, honey, it's me," Nicole said quickly. "Are you feeling okay?"

"What? Yeah, I'm fine. What's going on?" he said, sounding confused.

"Nothing, nothing. I'm sure it's nothing. It's just, I had a terrible feeling right now that something was really wrong, and it was really strong, so I wanted to call and make sure you're all right," Nicole said.

"Okay, well, I'm sorry you experienced that, but I'm totally fine."

"Definitely fine?" she teased.

"Perfectly fine."

"Okay, I'll leave you to your morning routine. I'm going to try to refocus on this report," Nicole said in a determinedly cheerful tone.

"Okay, feel better, love you, bye," her husband mumbled.

"Bye."

Maybe she'd make a fresh cup of coffee. That probably was not what she needed after that little jolt, but she felt like it might calm her nerves all the same.

Nicole walked to the little kitchenette near the main doors and put her mug under the spout of the fancy one-serving coffee machine. They used to use the one-use pods, but Nicole had campaigned for a switch, since those were so bad for the environment, and for the last six months they'd been using a machine that made single servings using real coffee beans spooned into the top of the machine. It was a small accomplishment, but she was proud of it. "Every little act helps," her mom always used to say. "None of it matters and I like my coffee the way I like it" is probably what her dad would say about it. Well, she had both of her parents in her.

The machine dinged. Nicole picked up her mug and walked back to her desk slowly, so as not to spill it. As she sat back down at her desk, she realized that her first reaction had been one of worry, but she had only thought of practicalities. She hadn't thought of God at all, hadn't instinctively prayed or anything. It had been a while since she'd thought of God, if she was honest with herself. She'd done all the rituals through childhood, including a blowout bat mitzvah party, of course. But her parents hadn't really gone to the synagogue as a religious thing—or at least if they had, they hadn't talked about it with her. It was more culturally important. And she really believed that. She'd gone to school with a mix of kids, but most of her close friends were also Jewish; it was just easier to have that cultural shorthand with them, to not have to explain things like she did to her non-Jewish friends who couldn't seem to remember what Rosh Hashanah was from year to year.

But God was a little different from that. Related, obviously, but not quite the same. Did she believe in God? She thought she did, and she prayed sometimes, but not really outside an official ceremony or service. She had felt very moved on her wedding day, when the rabbi was talking about the bond of marriage and what she and Aaron would mean to each other now that they were undertaking this solemn vow together. She probably felt the closest she'd ever felt to God on that day, gazing at her new husband with love and feeling how lucky she was. She spontaneously offered up thanks and felt her heart lift with it.

But after the wedding, life had very quickly gone back to normal. She and Aaron attended services together, and she lit the candles on Fridays, but she sang the words so quickly that she had no time to think about what they meant. The couple usually just wanted to sit down to dinner as quickly as possible. Her mother-in-law took it all a little more seriously, so when they were at her in-laws' house, Nicole exercised more patience. She could see the value in it, when Diane lit the candles and sang in her quiet, clear voice and said the words: "*Baruch ata Adonai, Eloheinu Melech ha-olam, asher kidshanu b'mitzvotav vitzivanu l'hadlik ner shel Shabbat.*" (Blessed are You, God, Ruler of the universe, who sanctified us with the commandment of lighting Shabbat candles.)

Nicole felt more centered and calmer when Diane sang, more ready to end the week and go into the next. She supposed she ought to consider this more. Was something missing in her life? Other than the baby that she tried not to wish for, maybe there was something else. Maybe she didn't quite have it all.

CHAPTER SEVENTEEN

G ail opened her eyes slowly. She felt fully rested, in a way she had not felt in a long time. *Part of that is probably the sex,* she thought, remembering the night before with fondness. Apparently, the oysters had worked their magic, because Jacob and Gail had fallen into bed entangled in one another's arms, and there wasn't even time to take off all her jewelry. She had gone to sleep wearing her new diamond pendant, and she reached down to her chest now, where it rested, warmed by her skin.

Suddenly Jacob's phone beeped. Gail rolled over and saw that Jacob was not beside her. The bathroom door was open, so he was not there either. Where had he gone? It was still early. She reached across the bed and picked up the phone.

Jacob where R you? Been 2 long. I miss you, she read. She checked the name: Claire Harris.

Gail calmly put the phone facedown on the nightstand, picked up a pillow, placed it over her face, and screamed.

How dare this woman be so blatant in her pursuit of a married man? How dare her husband encourage her? How dare both of them act like Gail was too stupid to know what was going on?

Gail thought again of last night, the way Jacob had looked at her when he told her she was the most beautiful woman in the world, the sincerity with which he'd said that he didn't even notice their server. She had believed him. Was she a fool? Was he making a fool of her and a mockery of their marriage, having an affair with a client who, from what Gail could remember, needed Jacob to defend her decision to cheat on her taxes? Was that the kind of woman he was attracted to? Apparently so; if she cheated on her taxes, why wouldn't she ask a man to cheat on his wife? Honor and duty meant nothing to her.

Gail threw the pillow aside and sat up. She needed some coffee. She used the hotel phone to call room service, ordered the fruit bowl with yogurt and a pot of coffee, and then got out of bed. She took the big, plush robe off the rack and tied the belt tight around her waist. She waited on the balcony, paging through a magazine and looking out over the hotel pool, purposely not thinking too hard about anything, until she heard the knock on the door. She thanked and tipped the young staff member (was everyone young here, or did she just feel old?).

When Jacob returned to the hotel room twenty minutes later, Gail was sitting on the suite's couch, drinking her second cup of coffee. She had thought she was feeling fairly calm, but as soon as the door closed behind him, she burst out angrily.

"You said it was over."

"What?" he asked.

Gail held up his cell phone. "She texted," Gail sniffed. Understanding dawned on Jacob's face, and he reached out for the phone, but she kept it in her hand.

"It's her number," Gail continued. "You said it was over. So why is she texting you? And how does she have your number anyway?"

"Gail, I give all my clients my cell number. You know that," Jacob said. "And I have told you, we had one drink. That was it. Nothing happened."

"Do you find her attractive?"

"Yeah, I do. I'm not going to lie," Jacob said.

"Oh, now's the time you find honesty?" Gail said.

"Gail, she is a very beautiful woman. But I am married, and nothing happened. I swear on my life. As God is watching!"

That surprised her. She could not think of a time when Jacob had invoked God in an argument. Perhaps he meant it. She hoped he meant it. Gail slowly set the cell phone on the couch next to her. She took a sip of coffee. Jacob cautiously sat beside her.

"Where were you, just now?" she asked.

"I woke up too early and went for a walk on the beach. It was a beautiful sunrise," he replied.

"Yes, I saw the last of it from here on the balcony. Alone," she could not help adding.

"I'm sorry. I didn't want to wake you. You looked so peaceful, and I thought a walk would do me good. Surely Lowy would be happy I got some exercise?" A half smile formed on Gail's lips.

Encouraged, Jacob reached out and held her hand. "I cannot wait to see tonight's sunset with you. Gail, let's forget about this and have a nice vacation. You put so much effort into it. I want you to enjoy it."

Gail looked down at their hands, the creases of age and the tan of a Southern California life, his wedding band glinting in the morning light. *This is what I wanted*, she reminded herself. She had not seen any messages from Jacob to Claire Harris. Maybe she was pursuing him, and he was fending her off. That was possible. She wanted it to be true. She wanted them to have a strong marriage again. *Try over and over*, she told herself.

Gail squeezed his hand and said, "All right, on one condition."

"Anything."

"You put that cell phone in your suitcase while we're here. No work. No other women."

"Done."

CHAPTER EIGHTEEN

Jacob sat by the pool and sipped on his scotch while Gail paged through a magazine on the sun lounger next to his. He looked over at her and smiled. She glanced up, smiled back, and returned to her magazine.

He thought back to the first vacation he and Gail had ever been on. On their honeymoon, they went to Paris because Gail had always wanted to see Paris. Jacob hated it. The old city was not built for people his size, and more than once he had banged his head on a low doorway. He had to suck in his stomach when they got in the elevator because it was literally one person wide. Who ever heard of such a small elevator? What was the point? And then there were the French, who, true to rumor, were very rude. Or at least they seemed that way to Jacob, who admittedly didn't try much beyond saying, "Excusez-moi" in an offended tone when a waiter didn't come to the table quickly enough. The weather was mixed, with a couple of rainy days and a couple of sunny ones. The food was okay; some of it was really good and some of it was suspect—he knew what escargots were, and he did not order them.

Gail had loved it. She had studied some art history in college, and she dragged him to an endless procession of museums. She tried to explain why certain paintings were beautiful, and why people still cared about the Mona Lisa. She enthused about the food and tried the escargots, the frog legs, anything the waiter recommended. She kept calling it the "City of Lights" and said over and over how lucky she was. She was young and in love, and she was in Paris. What more could she ask for?

Jacob was in love too, but even that early in life, he was too selfish to just give someone what they wanted without begrudging it them. He went to the museums with Gail, but he dragged his feet and asked how many more old paintings they had to look at before he could check out the wine in the museum café. He went to the fancy restaurants with her, but he read the menu in an intentionally terrible French accent, in an overloud voice, so all the tables around them could hear him mocking the food they were all about to eat. He didn't want to walk along the Seine but complained that a taxi cost too much.

Gail bore it all well, and as she was young, she probably did not think that this boded ill for the future. She just thought her new husband was a loveable grump. She did not think that he would turn truly sour and make it hard for her to enjoy things in the future.

They made passionate love in their hotel bed (which Jacob noted was actually a decent size, unlike everything else in the damn country). They spent every morning lying in bed, eating room-service croissants, and drinking coffee that even Jacob had to admit was pretty good. They talked about the past, and how much fun they'd had at their wedding, how beautiful it had been, how many people had been there. They talked about the future, and how they hoped for a child soon. All of Jacob's irritating comments from the day before would melt away in their bed in the morning.

Those were the best parts of the honeymoon for both of them. For Gail, this was proof that with a little prodding, Jacob could learn to love Europe and enjoy going outside of his comfort zone a little. For Jacob, it was proof that there was nothing good about Paris but for this one room, and that was a hell of a lot of expense for a few lazy mornings, which they could just as easily get in their California home or a Mexican resort hotel room.

When they flew back to California at the end of their Parisian week, Jacob told Gail that he did not want to go back to Europe. He explained his logic about the house in California and the resort in Mexico. He reiterated how annoying France was. He laid out his case like the lawyer he was, making his closing arguments. Gail, who hadn't even realized she was in a courtroom, couldn't compete, and the verdict went in his favor. They never returned to Europe.

Thinking about this now, Jacob felt a pang of regret. Sure, Paris was a dump, but other places over there might not be so bad. He knew for sure he'd like the food in Italy, for example. They had a big anniversary coming up in a couple of years. Maybe he'd mention it. He'd be the big man then. Gail would be so grateful.

Jacob drained his scotch and leaned back on the sun lounger, a smug smile on his face. Yeah yeah, so he'd kept his wife from a place she loved, but he was going to make up for it big-time. He had heard that there were cruises in the Mediterranean now. They could go on one of those, have a good time.

Gail asked what he was grinning at. Jacob just smiled and waggled his eyebrows at her.

The rest of the vacation passed by in a pleasant blur. Jacob and Gail relaxed on the beach, went to a luau, drove around the island, and took dips in the pool. Jacob never mentioned the strange man he met on the beach, or Laura, and he definitely did not say anything about the pain he'd felt in his chest. Gail wanted a real vacation, and he wasn't going to spoil it for her.

CHAPTER NINETEEN

Jacob shook his watch as he pressed the elevator button for his floor. No good. It was still stuck at 6:16. He promised Nicole he'd wear it, but it looked like he'd have to temporarily break that promise to get the thing fixed. *Isn't that just the way; you get back from vacation, and everything's a mess.* He hoped that wasn't the case in his office. He turned the handle on the door and walked in.

His secretary, Donna, smiled up at him as he entered the waiting area. His mind on the watch and the work he had to catch up on, Jacob barely managed a quick smile at her before he grabbed his phone messages from the box on Donna's desk and continued down the hall to his office. Donna followed.

"Well, you look tan and relaxed," she observed.

"Yep," Jacob said absentmindedly, shuffling through the phone messages and tossing the unimportant ones in the trash.

"That was a great birthday party," Donna continued. "Gail sure knows how to throw a party."

"Ah, thanks," Jacob muttered, turning his attention to the stack of mail on his desk.

"Did you get some nice presents?"

"Yeah." That seemed to be enough small talk, or maybe Donna knew she wasn't going to get more out of him, because she changed topics as she sat across from him.

"I separated most of your mail, so it should not take you that long to go through it."

"I see. That's fine."

"And I took it upon myself to grant counsel for Eisenberg a continuance."

Jacob frowned. "Why did you do that? We were set to go to trial next week."

"Well, their attorney had a death in his family, and he had to fly back East," Donna explained.

"So? Someone died. That's not my problem," Jacob countered. "I am not going to get paid until the house sells, and now I have to wait. Screw him!"

"Jacob!"

"What, he can send someone else to go to court."

"Are you serious?" Donna looked at her boss's scowling face and added, "Of course you are. But show some compassion."

"Okay, whatever," Jacob said, dropping the issue and returning to the mail, which to his annoyance seemed to be mostly bills.

Donna had worked for Jacob for nearly twenty years. She knew when she could get away with chastising him, and she knew when she needed to cheer him back up.

"I do have some good news," she said, pushing a strand of brown hair behind her ear. Jacob turned his attention to her again. "An arbitrator has been assigned to your lawsuit with Michael."

"That is good news. But why didn't you email me?"

"Gail made me promise to only contact you if there was an emergency."

"What does she know?" Jacob demanded. "She doesn't pay the bills. Anyway, who is it?"

"David Samuels."

"I don't know him," Jacob said dismissively.

"He's a retired judge who just relocated from Bakersfield," Donna recited from memory.

"I would too," Jacob snorted.

"Be nice."

"Why? You ever spend time in Bakersfield?" Donna had to smirk at that. "Anything else?" Donna's smirk disappeared, and she shifted uncomfortably in her seat.

"Your, uh, friend, Ms. Harris, called five times."

"Yeah, and she tried texting me in Hawaii," Jacob grumbled. "Gail saw the text."

"I thought you told her . . ." Donna began cautiously.

"I did. But she is not hearing me."

"Jacob, I don't like being in the middle of this," Donna said.

"You're not. I will handle it," Jacob said impatiently. "Anything else pressing?"

Donna took a deep breath and twisted her hands together in her lap.

"Well, don't get upset. Mr. Yoon."

"Who?" Jacob looked puzzled.

"Mr. Yoon. Edward Yoon. Two years ago, he had a terrible crush fracture."

"Oh yeah, I remember." Jacob nodded. "Some illegal ran a light and T-boned him. The driver had no insurance, but we collected through his UM. So, he got his money. What does he want from me now?"

"I don't know," Donna replied. "But he came by last week and said he only needs a few minutes to talk to you. I know how you feel about me making appointments, but he seemed desperate. So"—she swallowed nervously—"I said he could come by at two."

"Damn it, Donna, I'm already up to my neck in it. It's my first day back. Fine, whatever. If that's all?"

Donna left the room quickly, closing the door behind her.

Jacob leaned back in his chair and surveyed his office. It was a standard lawyer's office, bookshelves lining two of the walls, a big window behind him with a view of the sleek glass building across the road. Jacob's personal contribution to the décor was the brownish tinge to the ceilings and walls, from years of cigarette smoke. That and the general messiness. Files were stacked on either side of his desk and spread across the top of it. The chair Donna had been sitting on had a small stack of files squished in the back. Jacob smiled. It might be a mess, but it was all his.

He spent the rest of the morning opening his mail, writing checks, and returning calls. At one o'clock he realized he was hungry, so he went down to the building's cafeteria to get lunch. Sipping on an extra-large Coke, he brought his cheeseburger and fries back to his desk. He returned to the tasks at hand, muttering to himself that it was a good thing he'd come back when he did or the whole place would fall apart. He had moved on to his dessert of lemon meringue pie when his intercom buzzed.

"Mr. Yoon is here," Donna's voice said brightly.

"Send him back," Jacob instructed. He wiped his mouth and put his fork down.

Mr. Yoon entered the office unsteadily, using a three-pronged cane for balance. Jacob didn't move from his seat but pointed to a chair for Mr. Yoon to sit in.

"Mr. Abrams, thanks for seeing me," Mr. Yoon said, smiling.

"See you're still using the cane," Jacob said.

"Yeah, it helps."

Jacob offered no reply, and Mr. Yoon's smile faded.

"You have a question? Your case is closed," Jacob reminded him.

"It is not about my case," Mr. Yoon said.

"Oh," Jacob said, picking his fork back up and attacking the pie. "Well, I am very busy, and I am not sure how I can help you."

"It is about my mother. She has breast cancer. Her doctor says that it has spread, and her insurance is refusing to pay for her treatment."

"Why not?" Jacob asked through a mouthful of pie.

"This is where I need your help. I was hoping a letter from you would change their minds. You are such a fine attorney. If you could write to the insurance company—"

"That is not something I do," Jacob said abruptly, cutting him off.

"Mr. Abrams," Mr. Yoon pleaded. "I went through all the money from my settlement to help pay my mother's medical bills. It is all gone. I am only asking for a letter. I do have enough money to pay you for it."

"I am sorry, no," Jacob said, polishing off the pie and shoving it to the side of the desk for the cleaner to deal with later. He deliberately picked up a client file and started paging through it, ignoring Mr. Yoon as the man slowly rose to his feet and left the office, shaking his head in disgust.

CHAPTER TWENTY

Donna stood in the doorway of Jacob's office as he popped a Tums and grimaced.

"Are you all right, Jacob?" she asked.

"I am fine," he said gruffly. "What is it?"

"I'm leaving for the day—just wanted to say good night and welcome back. Oh, and to remind you, Gail wants you there by 6:30, so don't be late."

"Got it. I'm leaving in a few minutes anyway. See you tomorrow."

"Good night."

Jacob waited until Donna had gone before he rubbed his chest. Must have been those greasy fries at lunch that weren't agreeing with him. Everything felt uncomfortable, and he started to get a little clammy. He decided to call it a night.

As he turned the ignition on his car in the parking lot, he called Gail.

"Are you on your way?" she asked.

"Yeah, but I got to stop and get, ah, what is that pink stuff?"

"What are you talking about?"

"You know, you drink it when your stomach is on fire," Jacob said impatiently.

"What did you eat?" Gail prodded.

"I don't know. Fries and a burger," Jacob replied, loosening his tie and opening his collar.

"Not on your diet," Gail said severely.

"Look, I don't need a lecture. I need the name of the pink stuff, and I'll see you in a few minutes," Jacob said shortly, wiping his brow of the sweat running down.

"Pepto Bismol," Gail relented.

Jacob drove recklessly to the closest convenience store. Sweat pooled under his arms as he squinted in the harsh fluorescent lights and searched for the pink bottle in the small medicine section. Out of breath from the short walk up to the checkout, Jacob leaned heavily on the counter and handed the pink bottle and a twenty-dollar bill to the cashier.

"Do you need a bag for that?" the cashier asked, looking at him from the sides of his eyes, as if embarrassed by what he saw.

"What? Uh, no," Jacob said, blinking rapidly in the too-bright lights.

"Okay. That's $6.16 back to you," the cashier said. Jacob pocketed the change and receipt and carried the bottle back to his car.

He turned the car on and rolled down his windows, then tried to open the bottle. Of course, it had to be childproofed. *Why can't these damn manufacturers make a bottle you can fucking open?* His hands were now drenched in sweat, which didn't make it any easier, but finally he twisted the lid off. He threw back the bottle like it was a shot of scotch, then grimaced at the taste. When he'd drunk about a quarter of the bottle, he set it down, put the lid back on, and turned on the radio. The Lakers were playing the Heat tonight. That would be a good game. That would make him feel better and help him ignore the pain pulsing in his chest.

He shook his head, wiped his brow again, and pulled out of the parking lot. As he approached the intersection, the light was just changing from yellow to red, but Jacob drove through anyway. Suddenly, he saw a pedestrian in the crossing and slammed on the brakes.

The pedestrian approached his window, enraged. Jacob briefly closed his eyes, wishing away this moment, this pain, and this whole damn day.

"Are you crazy? You could have killed me!" the pedestrian shouted. He poked at Jacob's shoulder accusingly. At his touch, Jacob's chest exploded in pain.

He could barely form words but managed to choke out, "I am . . . so . . . sorry. I am just not, uh, feeling good."

He looked up at the pedestrian and was horrified to see the face of the LAX bartender and the stranger on the Hawaiian beach. The same long black hair, olive skin, and cleft chin. The same unreadable eyes.

"Sorry is not good enough. And there is no escaping your sins!" the pedestrian shouted. His pointing finger had become his hand gripping Jacob's shoulder. Jacob felt like his whole chest was being squeezed in a vise. His shirt was soaked with perspiration. His vision was blurry. All he could see was the shadowed eyes of this man, and all he felt was pain. He did the only thing he could think to do. He hit the gas pedal.

The car pulled away from the pedestrian, but the pain didn't disappear. Jacob was sure the man's hooded eyes had followed him, and he accelerated further, noticing too late that he was headed straight for a parked car. Slamming into it, and Jacob lurched forward. As his head sank into the airbag, he passed out.

The car clock blinked 6:16.

CHAPTER TWENTY-ONE

Gail was in a good mood. After she had insisted that Jacob put his phone away while they were in Hawaii, they had a wonderful time. They stayed mostly at the hotel and enjoyed everything it had to offer, although they did drive around the island a little too. Gail even went in the ocean while Jacob watched from shore. And he complimented her swimsuit.

They had come back just two nights ago; she did that on purpose so that Jacob could have a full day to recover before going back to work. A vacation after the vacation, as the saying went. She spent Sunday doing laundry from their trip, and he caught up on the basketball. They ate a simple fish dinner based on what they had been eating in Hawaii, and they went to bed early.

This morning, Gail sent Jacob to work with a big kiss and good wishes. He had promised to be home at 6:30 for dinner, and she promised to make one of his favorite dishes. She called Donna after lunch to remind her to remind him to be home on time, and then she returned to her day.

By 6 p.m., she had dinner nearly ready. She was chopping tomatoes for the salad when she got Jacob's call. She was disappointed to hear that he had gone for greasy food at lunch, and to hear that familiar grouchiness in his voice. Not a great return to work, then. Well, that was too bad. She was determined to carry some of the magic of vacation back into the real world. They might still be eating a restricted diet according to Dr. Lowy's instructions, but she had put on the diamond pendant she bought at the hotel store, and she thought they might curl up together on the couch after dinner and watch a movie.

She had just sat down at the table to practice folding the napkins in one of the shapes the hotel restaurant had used when suddenly Riley streaked across the room and leaped into her lap. He sat there, quivering.

"Riley! Whatever is the matter, sweetie?" The cat turned his head into her chest. She stroked his long fur and glanced at the clock: 6:16. "It's okay. He'll be home in just a few minutes. Then you can get all the snuggles you want."

She fussed with the napkin for a few more minutes but could not get it to resemble a swan. "It doesn't even look like an ugly duckling that might turn into a swan, does it, Riley?" she asked the cat, who had stopped quivering but remained in her lap. She folded the napkin as normal and gently placed the cat on the floor.

The phone rang.

"That had better not be Jacob telling me he's going to be late," Gail muttered. "He was on time not that long ago."

She hardly understood what was being said on the other end of the line. She heard "your husband" and "car accident" and "hospital." She gripped the counter and put her hand against her forehead, as if to force her brain to concentrate on the horrible words coming out of the phone.

Eventually, she picked out the name of the hospital Jacob was in. She turned the oven off, grabbed her keys and jacket, and raced out the door without even turning off the lights. Riley meowed piteously as she pulled the door shut behind her.

It was worse than she had thought. When she got to the hospital and said who she was looking for, the nurse gave her a sympathetic look and sent out another nurse to talk to her right away. Apparently, the reason Jacob had been in a car accident was that he'd had a major heart attack. He lost control of the car and plowed into a parked car. He was in surgery right now.

Gail's first thought was *Just like Dr. Lowy said*. She felt terrible, but the doctor had warned that a major heart attack was almost inevitable, given Jacob's size and diet, plus the cigarettes. Still, it had not seemed like a real possibility. Her husband, mortal? Jacob, weak? Impossible. It went against everything Jacob the self-made man believed in. To hear in cold, clinical terms just how weak he was made Gail cry.

The nurse led her to the waiting room outside where they did emergency surgeries. She brought Gail a small paper cup of water and went back to her duties. Gail looked dully at the cup. It was one of those cones, so she could not put it down, which she wanted to do. She looked around and saw no trash can. She would have to drink it. *A sneaky way to get people to hydrate*, she thought. Not unlike how she would trick Nicole into drinking something that wasn't just sugared water when she was younger.

Nicole! She had not told their daughter what was happening. Should she wait until they knew the outcome of the surgery? No, she deserved to be told right away.

Gail drained the paper cup and put it on the seat next to her, took a deep breath, and picked up her phone.

CHAPTER TWENTY-TWO

Nicole had decided it was time to explore her spirituality a little more. She brought it up to Aaron a couple nights after she had that weird electric jolt.

Over dinner, she said, "I've been thinking." Then she stopped, unsure of how to go on.

Aaron looked up from his fish and smiled. "Uh-oh," he said, "sounds dangerous."

"Well, maybe a little," Nicole joked. "I've been thinking about God."

"Oh?"

"I've been thinking that it's been a long time since I've given God any serious thought, and I think I miss having Him in my life."

Aaron set his knife and fork down and wiped his mouth with his napkin. He got a look in his eye, one that Nicole thought of as his "lawyer look," when he was about to start attacking an idea like it was on the witness stand.

"What brought this on?"

"You know when I called you a couple days ago? How I thought something was wrong? I realized I didn't pray to God or ask for help or anything, and I thought, if I did believe, truly believe, wouldn't I do that?"

"Would you? You might be too panicked to do anything."

"Maybe."

"What good would it do to pray in that moment? Would you expect God to spare you if something were really wrong?"

"No. Maybe. I don't know."

"Then why do it?"

"I think I'd find it comforting."

"And is comfort a good basis for a sense of spiritual connection to God?"

"I don't know, Aaron! This is what I want to figure out."

"Okay, okay," Aaron said, raising his hands in defeat. "I'm just asking."

"I know, but I haven't figured anything out yet. I have a lot of questions too," Nicole said, idly pushing her fish around her plate.

"So, who are you going to ask these questions? Are you going to visit Rabbi Eisel?" Aaron asked.

"I was thinking that might be a good idea, right?" She looked to Aaron for confirmation.

"Makes sense to me. God is the man's business, after all." He chuckled.

———

A few days later, the day after her parents returned from Hawaii, Nicole sat in Rabbi Eisel's office. She clutched her purse tightly in her lap. She was more nervous than she thought she would be. *And why should I be nervous? I haven't done anything wrong. Well, unless leaving it until your mid-twenties to turn your mind to God is wrong.* Maybe that was what worried her.

The rabbi prepared her coffee at the little machine by his desk, and as she watched him, she felt a sudden jolt run through her whole body, not unlike the one that had started her on this journey. She put her hand to her heart and felt it beating furiously. What was going on?

The rabbi smiled kindly at her as he handed her the coffee, and she shook herself a little to get back in the moment.

"Sugar?" he asked.

"No thanks, Rabbi," Nicole said politely.

"All right. So here you are. Nicole Abrams, now Nicole Green. It's been a long time since you've been in my office. I can remember your bat mitzvah like it was yesterday. You sang so beautifully."

"Oh, I don't know about that," Nicole said modestly. "Anyway, I was so nervous."

"Most young people are. It's a big day!" The rabbi smiled.

There was a pause, longer than was comfortable, and Nicole had the sense of being waited out, like she was in a meeting with a client who wasn't sure about doing business with her. All right; she could do those meetings, and she could do this one too. After all, she was the one who had sought it out.

"Rabbi," she began. He smiled encouragingly. "Rabbi, I have started thinking more about God, and I want to, I mean, uh . . ."

"That's a good place to start, thinking about Him," he said. Nicole laughed weakly.

"I don't really even know where to start, though," she said. "I think I believe in God, but I don't talk to Him, I don't really have a relationship with Him, and I'm not sure what that might look like. Is it too late?"

"Oh, it's never too late, Nicole," Rabbi Eisel said reassuringly. "And that relationship can look like a lot of things. The main thing is to open your whole heart to God. Sometimes, when we're starting to build a relationship, even just with another person, we hold back. Right? Maybe when you start dating someone, you hold a part of yourself back because you're worried about their reaction to secret parts of you, or you're worried that you two might not last very long."

Nicole nodded. Even though she and Aaron had known each other all their lives, she had still been cautious when they started dating.

"With God, it's the same. You're entering into a relationship. You need to trust that He's going to still love you even after you show Him your secrets, maybe sins you have committed or bad thoughts you've had. You need to trust that He's in it for the long haul, the same as you. You have to say, 'Here is my heart' and really mean it."

"That sounds hard," Nicole said.

"It can be," the rabbi admitted. "At least at first. Trying anything new can be scary, and starting a new relationship with the all-knowing God can be a little intimidating, sure. But it's worth it. You'll feel a sense of peace you can't really know otherwise."

"I wouldn't mind feeling that," Nicole said. "Where do you recommend I start?"

"Well, as you know, we've got a fair number of books in our history," the rabbi said. They both laughed since the Jewish religious literature tradition was incredibly rich. "We also have the Women's Club that meets every month. The next one is in a couple weeks if you want to come to that. Talk to some others who have some of the same questions you do. And finally, you can just start working on it yourself. Your own conscience is a good guide. What does God want you to do to live a good life? Are you doing those things? What do you need to change to realign yourself to God's purpose for you?"

"I think I'm doing okay, but maybe I need to look at some things again," Nicole agreed. She put her empty coffee cup down on the desk. "Thank you. This was really helpful."

"I'm so glad," Rabbi Eisel said. "We aim to please!" They both laughed again.

Nicole collected her purse and cardigan and stood up. As she headed for the door, the rabbi said, "And of course, if you need any further guidance, you know where to find me."

Nicole walked out to her car, feeling hopeful. Her phone buzzed, and when she picked it up, she heard her mother crying.

"It's your father," Gail said.

CHAPTER TWENTY-THREE

He was floating on his back, a bright light above him. But they were back home from Hawaii, so he couldn't be swimming there. *And wait, am I wearing some sort of clothing? Is that the chatter of tropical birds?* Jacob tried to focus on one bird that sounded familiar.

"He wakes up for a second and then goes back to sleep," said the familiar bird.

"That's normal. He is still pretty heavily medicated," said another bird he didn't recognize.

Medicine. Talking birds. Jacob struggled to open his eyes. Something was not right.

"Jacob, darling, you're okay. You're in the hospital," said the familiar bird, who, as Jacob blinked, came into focus as Gail. His wife.

He couldn't speak. He could only blink at her. He turned his head and saw Nicole and Aaron on the other side of the bed. He concentrated and managed a smile.

"We all love you. Try and get some sleep," Gail said.

He saw a shadow at the foot of the bed. The stranger. The cleft chin and hooded eyes of the bar, the beach, the intersection. Jacob's eyes widened in alarm as the stranger reached out for his hand. Jacob struggled to pull away from him, and Gail reached out to him.

The monitor sounded an alarm, and the small, bright room quickly filled with hospital personnel. Jacob grimaced as his chest tightened. The stranger advanced. Jacob heard Nicole crying. He fell back into floating, his hand reaching out for Gail's.

———

Two days later, Jacob sat up in his hospital bed, pillows piled comfortably behind him, a glass of water on the bedside table. Gail sat in a chair next to him, her hand on his. Dr. Lowy strode into the room.

"Well, look who's up!" he said jovially. "How are you feeling?"

"Could be better," Jacob said, smiling wanly. Dr. Lowy leaned over to peck Gail's cheek, then picked up Jacob's chart. "Have they had you walking around today?"

"Just for a minute," Gail filled in. "They also had him dangle his feet sitting up in a chair."

Dr. Lowy nodded approvingly and put his stethoscope in his ears. Gail smoothed Jacob's hand with hers as Dr. Lowy bent his head to listen to Jacob's heart.

"Okay, take a deep breath, Jacob," he instructed. "Again." Jacob inhaled shakily. "And again. And again." Jacob let his breath out noisily while Dr. Lowy removed his stethoscope. "Good. Heart sounds good."

Jacob leaned back on his pillows. Dr. Lowy asked Gail a question in a low voice, and she replied with a worried look. If he were feeling better, Jacob would have jokingly told them to plan their affair when he wasn't around. But he didn't even have the energy to do that.

"Jacob," Dr. Lowy said, turning back to him and speaking in a normal voice. Jacob frowned in concentration, knowing that what was coming was important. "You had a heart attack. When you first came into the hospital, you had almost ninety percent blockage in two of your arteries and almost one hundred percent in the left descending artery. So we put stents in to open your blockage." Jacob held his hand tentatively against his chest. "But the stents failed, and you had another attack. Much more serious than the first. So we opened your chest wall and took some grafts from your legs in place of your arteries to restore the blood supply. In layman's terms, what you had is called the widow-maker, because very few people survive such an attack."

"But I did," Jacob said, with some of his old bravado.

"You did. You must have a guardian angel watching over you," Dr. Lowy replied. "But what you have is only a Band-Aid. If you don't change your lifestyle, next time, well . . ."

Gail let out a little sob. Jacob turned his head to her.

"Are you listening?" she cried.

"Yes," Jacob promised. "So how long will I be in here?" he asked, turning back to Dr. Lowy.

"That depends on you and how well you do in rehab," Dr. Lowy said.

"Rehab!" Jacob exclaimed. "I have an eating problem, not a drug problem."

"Cardiac rehab. We need to exercise your heart," Dr. Lowy explained, rubbing the bridge of his nose. "But if you are a good boy, you could conceivably be back to work, modified work, in three months." Jacob started to speak, but Dr. Lowy held out a palm to stop him. "You now live under my rules, my laws, in my court. Do you understand?"

"I do," Jacob mumbled.

"I can't hear you," Dr. Lowy said.

"I do, all right!" Jacob said loudly. Dr. Lowy grinned, and Gail hid a smile behind her hand.

"Thanks. This feels so good," Dr. Lowy said, standing. Jacob rolled his eyes. "Oh, and Jacob, you may want to say thanks to the man upstairs." Jacob stopped mid-eye roll and inclined his head to indicate that he would think about it.

Gail came around the bed to give Dr. Lowy a hug.

"I'll check in on him later before I leave," Dr. Lowy told her. "But you need to go home and get some rest. He'll be fine." Gail managed a shaky smile.

"Thanks," she said.

Dr. Lowy turned back to Jacob. "By the way, did you ever fill that prescription I gave you?" Jacob could barely remember what he was talking about. Some sort of book. He shook his head. "Well, you have a lot of time on your hands, and as a get-well present, I will buy it for you." He left the room.

"What prescription?" Gail asked.

"Some book. I don't know. If I'm not allowed to work, I might go crazy, so I guess I'll read it," Jacob replied.

"That's the spirit," Gail said, patting his hand.

CHAPTER TWENTY-FOUR

The weeks that followed were the most difficult of Jacob's life. For a full four weeks, he wasn't allowed to do anything except the exercises at his cardiac rehab. He wanted to walk around like he used to, but he knew that he couldn't; even the gentle exercises at the rehab center left him out of breath—forget walking around his neighborhood.

He spent his days watching TV: *The Price is Right*, CNN, *The View*, *Ellen*, and *Judge Judy*. He often argued over Judy's decisions, but any time he raised his voice too loud, Gail appeared in the doorway of the living room, admonishing him to take it easy.

Gail was taskmaster in all ways. She kept Jacob on the strict diet prescribed by Dr. Lowy, she made sure he rested as much as possible, she took him to his cardiac rehab appointments, she helped bathe and dress him, and she worried over how much sleep he was getting. Jacob joked that she was the most attentive prison warden, and she pretended to be annoyed. Or at least, he was pretty sure she was pretending.

Nicole visited as often as she could, stopping by after work and making meals with her mother rather than cooking at her own home. Even Aaron came several times, watching Laker games with Jacob in the living room while the two women cooked in the kitchen. Jacob tried not to think too hard about the reason for the increased visits or the thaw in his son-in-law's icy attitude toward him, but late at night, when he was trying to sleep, he would place a hand on his heart and count the beats.

Finally, Jacob was deemed strong enough to begin a walking program, and his first solo walk was to the lake. He brought some seeds to feed Laker and tossed them in the water. Laker paddled around, swallowing the seeds, as Jacob ruminated on his close call.

"That was quite a scare, Laker. I almost checked out," he said, surprising himself with how shaky his voice sounded. He tried for a joke: "I would've missed the playoffs!"

Laker quacked and swam in a small circle, seeking out more seeds.

"I don't know. What do you think? Is there really anyone up there watching over us?" Jacob mused. Laker swam away, leaving Jacob holding half a packet of seeds, a thoughtful expression on his face.

That night, Jacob went home and opened the book Dr. Lowy had "prescribed." It was a children's book by Oscar Wilde, and it told the story of a giant who built a wall around his garden to keep the neighborhood children from playing in it.

One spring day he sees the children have snuck in through a gap in the wall and are playing in the garden. He sees the error of his ways and goes out to welcome the children. They are all afraid and run away, except for one child, who is trying to climb a tree. The giant gives him a boost and announces that he will knock down the wall. He does so, and from then on, the children play in the garden whenever they want, and the giant plays with them. He is sad, though, because the boy who climbed the tree is never seen again. One day, when the giant is old, he goes out into the garden and sees a new tree he has never seen before, and beneath it, the boy from all those years before. The giant greets him, and the boy tells him that because the giant welcomed him before, he would now welcome the giant to his own garden. The giant dies and the next day is found covered in blossoms.

Although "The Selfish Giant" was clearly a Christian fable, Jacob could ignore the religious part of the story and focus on the main message of being less selfish. He didn't think he was as bad as that giant, but he was man enough to admit that he could sometimes be so focused on his own goals that he didn't notice others. That was probably enough, right?

CHAPTER TWENTY-FIVE

The first month of Jacob's cardiac rehab, Nicole felt she hardly had time to breathe. She still went to work full time, getting in at seven as usual, but when she got off work at four, she drove to her parents' and cooked with her mother. She stayed for dinner and then went home, exhausted. Gail called her much more during the day, so she was juggling the usual stress of a highly competitive hedge fund company as well as the anxieties of her mother, who found herself thrust into this caretaking role.

The first night of this new reality, Nicole got home to find Aaron finishing Chinese takeout on the sofa. She collapsed next to him and burst into tears. Aaron quickly put his chow mein aside and held her in his arms.

"Oh, Aaron, it was terrible," Nicole sobbed. "Mom was so stressed, and it took us an hour to make a simple baked chicken because every time she heard a noise from the living room, she rushed in there to see what was wrong. And usually, it was just Dad talking to Riley or changing the channel, and he got more and more annoyed every time she came in, so by the time dinner was ready, he was in a terrible mood, and she was totally frazzled. We hardly talked during dinner. Dad just looked so glum."

Aaron rubbed her back and made soothing noises. Eventually, Nicole's sobs slowed to a few hiccups.

"It was hard to see your dad in that hospital bed," Aaron said. "I'd hoped that when you saw him back in the familiar surroundings of his own home, it might be easier. I'm sorry it wasn't."

Nicole sniffed and sat back on the couch. Aaron pushed her hair behind her ear.

"Aaron, I know you're mad at my dad, and you have every right to be," Nicole said. "I can't believe how he treated your father, either. But he's still my dad, and I love him very much. I need your support when I go to see him. I can't go if I'm worrying that it will upset you or thinking about how you don't like him."

"I'm such a stubborn fool," Aaron muttered, closing his eyes in pain.

Nicole raised her eyebrows at him questioningly.

"Nicole, you know I looked up to Jacob like he was a second father when I was growing up. I think that's why it hurt even more when he turned on my dad. I felt betrayed in more than one way. I'm still mad at him, and unless and until he apologizes, I don't know that I can forgive him. I know I should, I'm sure the rabbi would say I should forgive him, but right now I can't. But I still care about him, and I can't stand to see him in pain, or you, or your mom. I will support you when you go to see him, and I'll also come along sometimes, if that would help."

Nicole kissed him. "Oh yes, that would help," she said, starting to cry again.

"Come on, let's get you into bed. It's been a long day, and you're worn out," Aaron said, standing and holding out a hand to her.

"But your chow mein," Nicole protested.

"I'll come back and take care of it. Let's take care of you first," he said. Nicole took his hand and followed him gratefully.

CHAPTER TWENTY-SIX

Gail pulled into the line for the drive-thru pharmacy and put the car in park. Overcome with a wave of exhaustion, she let her head drop back on the headrest and closed her eyes. She had not been this tired since Nicole was an infant. At least that exhaustion had been offset by the joys of her newborn baby, and all the smiles and soft cuddles the two of them shared. This time was very different; she was caring for a grown man who resented needing help and offered no smiles or kind words of his own in return for the ongoing care Gail provided. He didn't bark at her the way he did at service personnel, but he called her a prison warden often enough that she had started to feel like one.

She did all the usual things she had always done as his wife—buy the food, prepare the meals, arrange for housecleaning, do the laundry—but now she added caretaking tasks: refilling and picking up his prescriptions, making sure he took the right medications at the right times, keeping track of doctor appointments and driving him to them, dressing and undressing him, supporting him physically to move from room to room. She had never trained to be a nurse, but she had seen Nicole through the usual childhood illnesses, so she knew the basics of what to do to keep a person comfortable when they were unwell. Still, she felt out of her depth nearly all the time. And never once did Jacob thank her. Not once. She might have felt invisible, except he seemed to see her whenever he had a complaint to make.

More often than she cared to admit, Gail called Nicole to talk through whatever anxiety she was experiencing or whatever frustrating behavior Jacob was exhibiting at the time. She knew it was not good to rely on her child like that. She should remain the parent in the relationship, no matter how close they were. But it was hard. Her own parents were gone, and her friends from the synagogue and charity circles were kind, but she did not feel she knew them well enough. She wanted to talk to Diane, who would surely have words of wisdom and a few jokes to lighten the mood. Gail's heart ached for the loss of her friend, but understandably they had not talked in a couple of years, and she did not think she could contact her. She was a little hurt that Diane had not reached out. Surely Aaron had told his parents what had happened. Yes, there was a rift between them now, but a heart attack was a serious thing. Could they not have called her to see how she was holding up? Perhaps that was unfair of her, and that would have been too much to ask. That did not mean she didn't think about it sometimes.

On her way home from the pharmacy, she checked the clock: 2:27. She had time for one stop if she was really quick. She really shouldn't, she knew that, but she really wanted to. She made a detour and pulled up to the boutique off the main street. As she walked into the store, she waited for that calm feeling to flood her, as it had so often in the past, before Jacob's heart attack. But nothing happened. She felt as tense as ever. This had been true every time she went into a clothing or jewelry store since the heart attack. She could not get the same feeling, but she kept going back, hoping that this would change. When it didn't, she got angry, and she bought clothes and trinkets almost out of spite. Spite at whom, she could not have said. Jacob, for being so sick? God, for letting him be so sick? Herself, for being so weak?

Gail left the store with a bag in hand and a receipt stuffed hastily to the bottom of her purse. It was 2:46. Just enough time to get home and make sure that Jacob took his three o'clock pills. Then she could start thinking about dinner. The medicines, meals, doctors, and worrying had her stuck in a never-ending cycle, and there was no way out. She would keep trying over and over.

CHAPTER TWENTY-SEVEN

After Nicole's conversation with Aaron about the situation at her parents' house, it was a little easier, as she felt him by her side, giving her strength. But she still felt overwhelmed, and it didn't help that Jacob was deep in a funk that he didn't seem able to shake himself out of. Dr. Lowy said it was common for men who'd had heart attacks to experience depression, as they suddenly felt just how mortal they were and were forced to show vulnerability in accepting help as their routines changed drastically. That certainly fit her dad to a T.

One night, Nicole left her mom chopping vegetables in the kitchen and went into the living room, where Jacob was in his chair as usual, frowning at the TV and absentmindedly petting Riley, who sat on his lap. Nicole picked up the remote and turned the TV off.

"Hey, I was watching that," Jacob said.

"Yeah sure, I could see you were really enjoying it," Nicole said.

"How do you know if I was enjoying it or not?" Jacob demanded.

"Just because I'm sick doesn't mean you can just decide what I can and cannot watch."

"Okay, Mr. Lawyer. I get it, you have rights!" Nicole joked. She got a small smile in return. The ice cracked, if not broken, Nicole decided to move ahead. She perched on the edge of the couch across from her dad and really looked at him.

He had looked better. Because he wasn't allowed to move around very much, he was pale and his skin puffed out from his body as he retained water and couldn't walk to shake it off. His tall frame stooped more, and it looked like his hair was graying a little. Nicole's heart squeezed, seeing the great giant of her youth shrunk to this human size.

"Dad," she said, "I know things are really hard right now."

"You're telling me," he said.

"I know, we're all helping out, but we're not experiencing it the way you are. That must be difficult. But, Dad, it's hard for us too. Mom is having a really hard time. She wants to help you, but you keep pushing her away; you keep trying to avoid the things you're meant to do. You have to meet her halfway."

"She certainly is an attentive prison warden," Jacob joked.

"Yeah yeah, but jokes aside, she's not a prison warden. She's your wife," Nicole reminded him. "And she could use a little consideration right now."

Jacob closed his eyes briefly, and when he opened them again, it looked like he had tears in them. "You're right, Nicole. I should be more appreciative. One of the lessons I should've picked up in temple, huh?"

Nicole was surprised to hear him reference religion, but she nodded and managed to say, "Yeah, I think that's one of Rabbi Eisel's big ones."

"Okay, kiddo, I'll try and do better. Now can I finish disagreeing with Judge Judy, please?"

Nicole laughed and handed him back the remote. She held his hand briefly as she did so, and he gave it a little squeeze.

"My angel," he whispered.

Nicole walked slowly out of the living room; she was still working behind the scenes in the family, but it was worth it if this was the result.

CHAPTER TWENTY-EIGHT

A couple months passed by, during which Nicole still came by to help her mother make dinner, but less frequently than she had been—only a couple nights a week. Aaron came with her, although now that it was the off-season, he didn't have a game to watch with Jacob, and he spent most of the time playing games on his phone while Jacob channel surfed.

One evening, Jacob decided it was high time he did something. After Nicole had kissed his cheek hello and gone into the kitchen to help Gail with dinner, Jacob began the arduous process of rising from his chair. Aaron rushed over to lend an arm to steady him, and Riley mewed anxiously as Jacob unfolded himself into a standing position.

"Are you all right, Jacob?" Aaron asked anxiously.

"Oh yeah, this is how it works now. Standing up is a whole affair," Jacob laughed. "But it's got to be done so I can do my exercises. Speaking of which, I have left my walk a little late today. Do you mind going with me down to the lake?"

A look of surprise flashed across Aaron's face, but he covered it with a nod. "Yes, of course. Let me just let the girls know."

Gail and Nicole followed him out of the kitchen, fussing and tutting over Jacob's outfit and making sure he would be warm enough.

"All right, all right, he can dress himself," Aaron said.

"Thank you! I certainly can," Jacob said with great dignity. Gail and Nicole shared a quick smile. Aaron took Jacob's arm, and the two of them made their way to the back door. Riley wound himself between Jacob's legs.

"Sorry, Riley, it's just us two guys. We'll be back soon for dinner," Jacob said.

"Come here, Riley," Nicole said, bending down and scooping him up. "Let the guys have a walk. We'll stay in here and have a pre-dinner glass of wine."

"That sounds more like it," Gail said.

The two men shuffled down the path slowly. Aaron was very conscientious, taking small steps and pausing any time it looked like Jacob might be out of breath.

"Looking forward to next season," Jacob said.

"Yeah, they're in a great position," Aaron agreed. "Definitely gonna be champs this year."

"Definitely." Jacob stopped and coughed. Aaron gripped his arm more tightly, and Jacob leaned into him.

"Thank you," he said. "Aaron, this is tough for me to say, but—"

"You don't have to if you'd rather not," Aaron said, a little stiffly.

"No, I need to," Jacob said. "I should have said this a long time ago. Aaron, I'm sorry for the way I treated your dad. Michael has been a good friend to me for more than half my life now, and in a moment of madness I treated him terribly. I think . . . well, I think it was mainly jealousy. He was going for a judgeship, and I was going to be left as just a lawyer. 'Just' a lawyer! I love my job, always have. I don't even want to be a judge. That's not for me. But your dad would be perfect at it. He's got the right temperament, and he's more fair-minded than me."

Jacob risked a glance at Aaron to see how he was taking this. Aaron avoided eye contact but kept his arm out for Jacob to hold on to.

"So, I backed Weiner and siphoned off clients in case backing Weiner didn't work and your dad won anyway. I did it out of jealousy and out of greed. Those clients stayed with me when we split up, and I have continued to make a lot of money off of them. And in the end, your dad didn't become a judge, and I know that has something to do with me, and I'm ashamed of it. If he ever runs again, I'll be the first to support him."

"That's good to hear, Jacob," Aaron said. "Thank you for saying that." They started moving again.

"Aaron, I hurt your dad, and I hurt everyone else too. Your poor mother, who was never anything but kind to us, and Gail, who misses Diane and Michael every day. And of course, you and Nicole. You two had just been married, and everything seemed so good. But maybe, maybe—" Jacob stopped suddenly, as if it was too much to go on. Aaron rubbed his back encouragingly. They reached the bench by the lake and sat.

"I don't know, Aaron. I have always loved you; I've known you your whole life. I am so happy that you and Nicole are together, as I must admit all of us hoped you might be one day. But I think it's possible that even though I am happy for you two, a part of me was also upset that my baby was leaving. Maybe I was almost mad at you without knowing it, and that was part of why I lashed out . . . Oh, I don't know. Now I'm talking psychobabble nonsense, but I have been trying so hard lately to think of why I did what I did, and I'm clutching at straws."

Aaron nodded quickly, like he was trying to take it all in, but it was too much. He blinked back tears. Jacob started crying, and he reached out a hand to place on Aaron's cheek.

His voice dropped to a whisper. "Aaron, I am so sorry for what I did to your family. I know I don't deserve forgiveness, but I am asking for it anyway. If you can find it in your heart one day, I would be more grateful than I can say."

Aaron turned his head so that Jacob's hand fell away from his cheek. The Adam's apple in Aaron's throat bobbed up and down as he swallowed. Jacob wept quietly and let his hands sit in his lap. Laker the duck swam up and quacked at Jacob, turned in a couple circles, and then swam away again when he realized he was getting no seeds today.

Jacob was just starting to think that this had been a huge mistake when Aaron spoke. His voice was low, and he talked to the lake rather than risk looking at Jacob.

"Thank you, Jacob. I know that was hard for you to say. It was incredibly hard to hear. I don't know that I can forgive you right now, but I want to be able to. Your apology is sincere, and that is all I need to be able to work toward forgiveness." He turned his head so he was facing Jacob. His voice cracking, he said, "I've loved you like a second father my whole life, and it killed me to see you treat us like that. It really shook my faith in people, that someone I loved and trusted could do something so wrong. Luckily, I have Nicole, who as you know is one of the most trustworthy people in the world, and one of the kindest. She has pulled me through so that I am not as bitter as I might be otherwise."

"Yes, she really is the best of us," Jacob agreed.

"Will you be talking to my father?" Aaron asked. Jacob took a ragged breath.

"I will. I don't have the courage just yet, but I'm going to soon. He deserves an apology. And I miss him so much."

"I know he misses you too," Aaron said quietly. He reached out and gripped Jacob's shoulder. Jacob placed his hand over Aaron's. The two sat there for a very long time, until Nicole had to come find them and bring them in for dinner.

CHAPTER TWENTY-NINE

The first month of Jacob's rehabilitation had been the worst for everyone, including Gail. But toward the end of that time, when Jacob was given the go-ahead to slowly start exercising, her grumpy patient changed his tune a little. He didn't say anything to her about how he had been feeling or apologize for his bad behavior, but he stopped complaining so much. He complimented her cooking and declared he had a favorite out of the selection of healthy new recipes she was now making. And he did not call her a prison warden anymore. Gail did not know what brought on this change, although she suspected that their daughter, ever the peacemaker, may have had a word with him. Well, if she had, that was kind of her, and even better, it had worked.

For the next few months, Jacob and Gail both got more comfortable in their roles and routines. Gail still performed her housekeeping and caretaking duties, but Jacob was more receptive to them, so they didn't feel like so much of a burden. Plus, now that he was allowed to move around more, Jacob was regaining some of his old energy and taking longer and more frequent walks around the lake.

The first time he went by himself, Gail thought she would be the one to have a heart attack, she was so nervous. What if he fell? What if he had an attack out there? What if his slow shuffle landed him in the water and he couldn't get out? What if he somehow snuck a cigarette while he was out there?

"What if, what if," Jacob had said. "What if I never leave this house again? I think that is the thing you really need to worry about!" He said it with a smile and a pat on her backside, so Gail smiled back at him and agreed to let him go.

He shuffled out the back door, a packet of seeds in his pocket for the birds, and she waved and forced herself to smile and say, "Have a good time." But she watched him until he was out of sight, and even then, she remained on the back porch, hugging her elbows, worry creasing a frown in her forehead. She tried to distract herself by trimming back some of the bushes in the yard, figuring that she would be that much closer if he was suddenly in trouble, but it was no good. She could not concentrate on the task and found herself constantly straining to hear any sign of him.

When he did finally return—a mere twenty minutes later, although it felt like a week to Gail—Jacob was out of breath, and his face had a sheen of sweat from the effort. Gail nervously rubbed her thumb against her engagement ring to keep from running up to offer help. She knew it was important to him to do this all by himself. She was rewarded for her restraint when he made it up to the back door and turned to smile at her.

"So that's what you can do with your what-if!" he said happily.

"I guess so," she agreed, leaving the clippers on the picnic table and joining him. She pecked him on the cheek. "What if we go inside and have some of that sugar-free lemonade?"

"All right," he consented.

It was not long before Jacob was taking daily walks down to the lake. He told Gail about his favorite duck, one with a purple stripe that he had named him Laker. It was a small thing, but this sign that her basketball-loving husband had not lost all his interests cheered Gail. She made sure there was always birdseed available for Jacob to take down for Laker and the other ducks.

The other good part about the routine they all settled into was that Nicole and Aaron came over for meals—not every day like in the beginning, but a couple times a week. Gail cherished these family meals, which they had not had in so long. It was good to see Nicole and Aaron together, a rare thing over the last two and a half years.

Best of all, Aaron and Jacob seemed to have reached a détente. One evening, Jacob took Aaron out for his walk down to see Laker, and Nicole and Gail stayed back at the house, chopping vegetables and having a small glass of wine each. Mother and daughter wondered about what was going on down there, but the men were mum when they came back, so the women wisely left it until each was alone with her husband to press the issue.

Jacob said that he had apologized to Aaron for freezing him out and for treating his father so badly. It was one of the hardest things he had ever done, he said, but he was glad he had.

"Did he accept your apology?" Gail asked.

"Sort of. He said he would have to consider whether he could forgive me."

"What do you think of that?"

"Oh, I think it's fair," Jacob said with a weariness that belied his earlier cheerful attitude. "I have behaved abominably to everyone, and I know it. I practically helped raise him, and then I turned around and did that. I can see how that might make it hard for him to trust me again."

Gail rubbed his shoulder and placed her other hand on his cheek.

"I'm proud of you for talking to him, Jacob. I know that was not easy, but it is such a good sign that you took that step."

Jacob smiled at her. "Remember in Hawaii, how you told me I had to be more grateful for what I had? I am so grateful for you."

Tears sprang to her eyes. "Thank you. It's wonderful to hear that," she said softly.

"I should say it more often, then." Jacob embraced her, Gail's petite body tucked into his giant frame. Even though his body had changed a lot in the last few months with the heart attack and diet changes, he still felt solid as he held her.

CHAPTER THIRTY

A couple months later, Jacob went in to Dr. Lowy for a checkup. His blood pressure was way down, he'd lost thirty pounds, and his diet and exercise regime seemed to be working. The doctor declared that Jacob was making his work boring, and that he could return to the office the following week. After a short conversation that embarrassed the two friends, he sent Jacob home with a few samples of Viagra, to counteract some side effects of the heart medication.

That night, as they were getting ready for bed, Gail put a small jewelry case on Jacob's dresser. He opened it and found his Lakers watch, now working properly.

"The repair guy said he's never seen anything like it," Gail said as Jacob kissed her cheek. "The minute and hour hand froze. He said it was like the watch was hit by lightning and time stopped right at 6:16."

Jacob shook his head and gave the watch a little pat before putting it aside for the night.

"Thank you for having it fixed," he said.

"You are welcome," Gail said, pleased. "I wanted you to have it in working order when you returned to work." Jacob reached over and kissed her again, this time on the lips.

"You are so good to me," he murmured. "Why did you ever marry me?"

"Because," Gail replied, her hands slowly unbuttoning his shirt, "my mother said that deep down, very deep down, you were a good, kind person who would adore me and protect and provide for me."

"I do want to be that person," Jacob said, kissing her neck. "I'll try harder."

"Good," Gail said. "Oh, and there is another reason I married you."

"What's that?" Jacob asked, leading her to the bed.

"Those beautiful brown eyes and that adorable smile," she said. He flashed that very smile at her and lowered himself on top of her. Gail felt his arousal against her thigh.

"Mr. Abrams. Welcome home."

CHAPTER THIRTY-ONE

Jacob approached the courtroom nervously. He'd been away for a long time. What if he'd lost it? What if he was no longer the great criminal lawyer he'd worked so hard to be? He straightened his tie and immediately felt better. His suit was new, a slimmer fit that flattered his trimmer body. *I can do this*, he thought.

The jury was already seated to his far left, and to his immediate left, at the other counsel's table, he recognized the district attorney. The bailiff announced the judge, and everyone rose to their feet. A judge Jacob didn't recognize entered the courtroom and took his seat.

"Mr. Abrams," the judge said. "You may proceed."

"Ladies and gentlemen," Jacob began.

"Mr. Foreman," the judge said, cutting him off, "has the jury reached a verdict?"

The jury foreman stood. "We have, Your Honor," he said.

He looked vaguely familiar. What was going on? Jacob remained standing.

"Your Honor, I am confused. What's going on here? I have not yet presented my case," he said, gesturing to the notes in his hands.

"Mr. Abrams, the court has heard your argument far too many times," the judge said. "Your fate is now in the hands of the jury."

Jacob looked down at the yellow legal pad in his hands, searching for an explanation somewhere in his notes. A trickle of sweat started its way down the nape of his neck. He looked up at the judge and saw he was now wearing a white suit and looked somehow bigger and more imposing than before.

But more terrifying was the sight of the stranger who had been haunting him, now sitting across the table from him. His hair was loose around his shoulders, and he was wearing an impossibly black suit, so black it seemed all color was sucked into it. His eyes were hooded as usual, and there was no mistaking that cleft chin. The stranger stared at him impassively as Jacob sat back in his chair, gasping.

"Go ahead, Mr. Foreman," the judge said.

"Your Honor, I insist," Jacob said weakly, although he knew now that he had no case to present. The stranger slowly pointed a finger at him.

"Silence!" commanded the judge. Jacob felt dizzy.

"We the jury find the defendant, Jacob Abrams, guilty of lust, gluttony, greed, sloth, wrath, envy, and pride," the foreman intoned.

"Your Honor!" Jacob leaped to his feet. The stranger started laughing.

"Mr. Abrams, I told you to be quiet. Sit down. I will now poll the jury," the judge said.

Jacob stared at the jury and was astonished to find that he knew each face in that jury box. He held a hand to his chest as everyone in his life shouted out their verdict on him.

"Juror number one, Mr. Foreman," said the judge.

"Guilty," said Dr. Lowy.

"Juror number two."

"Guilty," said Gail.

"Gail! Sweetheart!" Jacob cried out. But she turned her face away from him.

"Juror number three."

"Guilty," said Nicole.

"Juror number four."

"Guilty," said Aaron.

"Juror number five."

"Guilty," said Michael.

"Michael, I am so sorry," Jacob sobbed.

"Juror number six."

"Guilty," said Donna.

And so it went through all twelve jurors: Mr. Woo, Dr. Lowy's receptionist Cindy, the hotel desk clerk from Hawaii, the man begging for money at the freeway exit, people from even further in his past. Jacob sobbed and begged them to change their verdict.

He looked up in horror as the stranger stood, smoothed his black suit, and walked toward him.

"What penalty does the jury impose upon Mr. Abrams?" the judge asked.

The entire jury rose to their feet and, pointing at him, shouted as one: "Death!"

The stranger reached out to grab him, his dark eyes revealing nothing. The faces of those in his life were twisted in anger.

"No, no, no!" Jacob screamed. "No! Please!"

"Jacob. Jacob. Wake up, Jacob!" Gail shook his shoulder.

"What?" Jacob eyes flew open, and he looked around wildly.

"You're having a nightmare," Gail said soothingly.

"I am? Where? What?" Jacob clutched at his wife. She stroked his arm.

"You're okay, Jacob," she reassured him. Jacob's heartbeat slowed, and he took a deep breath. "It was a bad dream, but you're all right," Gail said. She peered at the nightstand clock. "Go back to sleep. It's only 6:16."

—————

The next day, Jacob sat on the couch alone, petting Riley, who purred contentedly. Jacob had been watching *Judge Judy* for an hour already and wasn't sure he wanted more. Gail was out buying groceries. He was going back to work in two days. He was restless, and still a little shaken up from his nightmare the night before. He started channel surfing.

One of the channels showed an evangelist preaching something, but Jacob didn't pay attention to that. What caught his attention was what flashed across the bottom of the screen: "Proverbs 6:16." Jacob froze. Suddenly, there was no sound in the room at all—not Riley purring, not the evangelist preaching, not even the hum of the refrigerator in the kitchen.

Jacob turned off the TV and slowly got to his feet. The normal sounds of the house returned, but the strangeness and importance of the moment hadn't left him. He repeated the numbers out loud to himself: "Six, sixteen, six, sixteen, six, sixteen . . ."

As he did so, images fluttered into his mind, slowly at first, and then in a deluge. The airport noticeboard for flight 616. The hotel room sign reading 616. The change from the Pepto Bismol, $6.16. The brand-new watch from Nicole, mysteriously stopped at 6:16.

"Oh no, even the courtroom from my nightmare was Department 616," he remembered aloud. Riley mewed questioningly.

Jacob hurried over to his desk and opened his computer. He googled "Proverbs 6:16." The top result quoted from the Bible: "There are six things that the LORD hates, seven that are an abomination to him: haughty eyes, a lying tongue . . ." Jacob couldn't read anymore. He felt dizzy and his vision blurred. Worried about another heart attack, he clutched at his chest, but he was fine. He took a deep breath. This was a different kind of attack, an attack on his sins. He could finally read the signs.

CHAPTER THIRTY-TWO

Everything about Rabbi Eisel's study seemed old fashioned. The walls were lined with floor-to-ceiling bookshelves, the desk was a broad expanse of mahogany, the chairs a mix of hard-backed and overstuffed. Even the rabbi himself wore wire-rimmed spectacles instead of the trendier plastic frames of today. Where Jacob's office had piles of client files on every available surface, the rabbi's study was bursting with books.

"Jacob, so nice to see you," Rabbi Eisel said. "Sit, sit."

Moving a small pile of books onto another chair, Jacob sat down. The rabbi settled into his seat behind his desk.

"How are you feeling?" he asked. "I saw Gail yesterday at the meeting and she said you are doing great."

"I am," Jacob acknowledged. "Back to walking, watching my weight. I've lost thirty pounds."

"That must be difficult. That Gail of yours is an amazing cook," the rabbi noted.

Jacob smiled. "She is." Rabbi Eisel poured them each a coffee from the machine next to his desk—just about the only modern thing in the room. Jacob accepted his cup with a nod. "Thank you, and thank you for visiting me in the hospital."

"Of course," Rabbi Eisel said. He paused, stirring sugar into his coffee. "So, Jacob, when was the last time you were here?"

"Are you really asking me, Rabbi?" Jacob said.

"No. I know. You and Gail sat here with Nicole, and we talked about her bat mitzvah. What year was that?" He peered over his glasses at Jacob.

"I don't know, Rabbi," Jacob said in a small voice.

"I can tell you. It was 2006. I may be old, but I don't forget. I can remember every child. So, how can I help you?"

Jacob turned the coffee cup around and around in his hands. "Rabbi, I know this sounds crazy, and I wouldn't want anyone to hear—"

"Jacob," Rabbi Eisel said, "you are an attorney, and you have, ah, what is it called? Attorney-client privilege. Well, we have the same thing. Anything you tell me is between you, me, and . . ." He looked up to the ceiling, indicating God.

"Really?"

"Sure, we Zoom every night," the rabbi joked. They both laughed, and Jacob felt some of the tension leave his shoulders. "So, talk to me."

"Well, I think . . . I mean, I don't know. I know I am not crazy. But I have read that sometimes, after a person has a heart attack, their mind starts playing games with them. You get confused with reality and what you may have dreamed. It could also be the medication I'm on. But—"

"So, you think God is talking to you?" the rabbi asked gently.

"I don't know about talking," he said cautiously. "I'm not hearing voices. But maybe sending messages." Abruptly, Jacob put his coffee cup on the desk and continued in a brisk voice, "Anyway, Rabbi, this is stupid, and I am sorry to waste your time."

He reached into his jacket pocket and pulled out his checkbook.

"Jacob," the rabbi said quietly, "I am not going to turn away your generosity. But you are not here just to deliver a check."

Jacob kept his face expressionless, a trick he'd mastered for the courtroom, but inside he was quivering. He felt he was on the edge of something important but terrifying. He didn't know if he could face it. He knew the rabbi would be honest with him, but what if his honest opinion was that Jacob was beyond hope?

"Talk to me, Jacob," the rabbi requested. Jacob swallowed, then sat up straighter in his chair, setting his shoulders back.

"Rabbi, I have not been the best person I can be. I know that. I have hurt people. People I love. And now. Now . . ." Jacob's eyes filled with tears, and his voice started to shake. "Now I think God is punishing me for my sins."

Rabbi Eisel smiled supportively. "Jacob," he said, "if you have sinned, there is still time to repent. God will lead you on the path." Jacob bowed his head, grateful for the rabbi's kind words. "In fact," the rabbi continued in a brighter tone, "your timing could not be better."

The rabbi moved some books aside on his desk and picked up a flyer. He held it out to Jacob.

"Here. I want you to come to my next class."

Jacob looked down at the flyer. The first part of it jumped out at him: *Proverbs 6:16 – Repenting Sins and Practicing Virtues for a More Extraordinary Life.*

CHAPTER THIRTY-THREE

The day Jacob returned to work, Gail made him a lunch: a sandwich with the low-sodium turkey he liked, a big salad in a Tupperware container, and an apple. She felt nostalgic making it, remembering all the lunches she had made for Nicole when she was a child. She was also nervous, sending Jacob back into the world. She trusted Dr. Lowy's opinion, and if he said Jacob was ready to go back, then she believed him. But like mother, like daughter; Gail was a worrier. She worried the work would be too much, even though Donna promised she had cut his caseload down to a manageable size. She worried he would be too tempted by the fast food and cigarettes easily available out there, although Jacob had promised that he would stay away from them.

Jacob appeared in the kitchen, dressed in his favorite work suit, briefcase in hand.

"Ta da!" he said and did a slow turn. Gail laughed.

"Very nice," she said. "Come here; let me straighten that tie. And call me on your way home. I'm making that chicken dish you don't hate."

They both laughed. Jacob's begrudging acceptance of his new diet was now a joke between them.

"Can't wait. Thanks for lunch," Jacob said, grabbing the bag. "Love you."

"Love you."

And just like that, he was gone.

Gail did the breakfast dishes, got the chicken out of the freezer for dinner that night, changed Riley's litter box. She had gotten used to the new routine where Jacob was at home, and now that he was gone again, she felt at loose ends.

There was something she could do, something she had not done in months. After that early trip to the boutique on the way home from a prescription run, she had not taken any shopping trips. The bag from the boutique sat in the back of her closet, and she probably still had the receipt stuffed in the bottom of her purse if she wanted to look for it. It sat among at least a dozen other bags, all from high-end stores, all unopened, sitting there as a silent testament to the shame Gail felt for making these purchases over and over.

She put on her spring jacket and grabbed her keys.

"I'm just going to see," she said to Riley, who had trotted in when he heard the keys. "I want to see if the urge is still there."

When she got to her favorite little store, tucked away on a side street with not much traffic, Gail cut the engine and unbuckled her seat belt. She tried to take a few deep breaths. What if she went in there and the thrill was still there? What if it wasn't, and she got angry and bought things she didn't need out of anger? What if the years of playing the role of a bored housewife had actually turned her into one, and she was now hopelessly materialistic? What if her attempts to recenter her life on being a good person, a good wife and mother, were all for nothing?

Suddenly, she heard Jacob's voice in her head—"That's what you can do with your what-if!"—as he came back from his first walk to the lake by himself since his surgery. Gail laughed. She was getting herself worked up, and the only way to know for sure if she was okay now was to take the next step.

As she crossed the threshold, Gail did not feel any different. She didn't feel less tense, but then, she had not been very tense before. She didn't feel more tense, either. She felt fairly neutral. This seemed a good sign. She wandered around the store, smiling at the salesperson who indicated her readiness to assist. Gail made sure not to rush but to linger if she wanted, to feel the soothing influence of the calming music and the gentle lighting. She held silk blouses up to look at them in the light, asked the salesperson to take out a few bracelets for her to try on, slipped her feet into three different pairs of heels. As she did all these things, she noticed that she felt fine. She did not feel a rush of adrenaline; she did not feel out of control or angry. She felt calm, like she could appreciate being in a nice store, trying on nice things, but not like she needed to take them home and hide them from view. She returned to the door, thanked the salesperson for her assistance, and walked back to her car. She felt free.

————

That night at dinner, Jacob commented on how nice the meal was, then cleared his throat.

"Gail, I want to—I mean, I need to . . ."

"What is it, Jacob?"

"Gail. I didn't tell you, but I had a meeting with Rabbi Eisel."

"The rabbi? Are you okay? What's wrong?" *I knew it was too early for him to go back to work!*

"No, no, I'm fine, I'm fine, really," Jacob reassured her. "Physically, I feel fine. But spiritually, I have been feeling not my best lately. Well, for a long time now, but I have only lately come to see the truth of that. I let myself fall into sinful ways, and they have done nothing but hurt my family, and my own soul."

"Jacob—"

"No, please wait. I talked to the rabbi because I wanted to know if he thought God had time for me anymore, given that I have not made time for him in decades."

"I'm sure he does," Gail said gently.

"The rabbi agrees with you," Jacob said. "There's this class at synagogue going on for a few weeks, focused on the seven deadly sins. I can count myself sinning on just about all of them, so it sounds like a good thing for me to go to. But I'm scared, Gail. I'm scared to face my failings. Will you go to the classes with me? I would really appreciate your support."

Gail thought of her own struggles in the last few years—the impulsive shopping trips, the uncharitable thoughts toward her husband. This class could be good for both of them.

"Of course I'll go with you."

CHAPTER THIRTY-FOUR

It was a beautiful day, the kind that made Nicole glad to be alive. The LA sun shone down, but a light breeze coming in from the ocean kept it from getting too hot. She jogged down the park trail at a steady pace, her blond hair bouncing.

Things were going well lately. Her dad had lost some of the weight Dr. Lowy wanted him to, he'd gone off the booze and the cigarettes, and he enjoyed his daily walks down to the lake near his house. Her parents seemed to be in a good place, and her mother was less stressed when she talked to Nicole on the phone. Nicole and Aaron still went over after dinner every few nights, and now that Jacob had apologized to Aaron, the dinners were less strained.

She had been enjoying the Women's Club meetings at the synagogue, too. It was a small group, about ten or so—mostly retired women, as the meetings took place on Thursdays at 5 p.m. The timing was okay for Nicole since she could just skip lunch and still get a full day's work in, but it wasn't a great time for other working women, or women who had to pick their kids up from school. Most of the women she knew vaguely from going to temple, but now that they were spending time together, she got to know them much better, and they her.

She got along particularly well with Rachel, who was in her seventies and a grandmother several times over. The two of them shared a sense of humor, and Rachel always knew the right thing to say. At the last meeting, after one of the other women had gone on for a while about her new grandson and how much joy he brought her, Rachel noticed Nicole's quietness. She came over and put a soothing hand on her back.

"It's not always easy to hear of the joys of others when we wish those joys for ourselves, is it?" she asked gently.

"Oh, was I that obvious? I tried not to be," Nicole said.

"No, dear, but you've talked in the past about wanting a baby but it not being the right time for you and your husband, so I was aware that it was something of an issue. Do you want to talk about it?" Rachel took out the knitting she always carried with her, tucked a needle under her arm, and started counting stitches.

"Well," Nicole began uncertainly. She wasn't sure she should air the dirty laundry of her family to this woman she didn't know that well. Perhaps she could phrase it in a way that did not incriminate anyone. *Here I am, thinking like a lawyer again!* she thought wryly.

"Well, you see, I am married to a childhood friend. Our fathers were in business together until a few years ago."

"Oh yes, Jacob Abrams and Michael Green—is that right?" Rachel asked. Nicole winced. *She might know the whole story anyway.*

"Yes, that's right. They are no longer friends. Do you know about that?"

"I try not to listen to gossip, dear. I heard they were no longer speaking, but I do not know the reason why," Rachel said. Nicole breathed a sigh of relief.

"You can understand I don't want to go into too much detail

about it, but suffice it to say, my father did something that hurt my husband's father, and now they aren't speaking, and my husband is too upset to think about having children."

"Oh my," Rachel said. "I can see that is a tricky situation. Is there any chance they will reconcile?"

"They may," Nicole said. "There is hope that a reconciliation might happen soon. But if they don't, how long can I wait for my husband to get over his anger before I can ask again for a baby?"

"Hm, I don't know, dear," Rachel said. "That's quite the conundrum. I can see why the subject is painful for you." Rachel knitted meditatively for a few moments, and Nicole sat quietly, her hands shaking around the teacup in her lap.

"Have you quoted Ezekiel to him? 'The son shall not suffer for the iniquity of the father, nor the father suffer for the iniquity of the son. The righteousness of the righteous shall be upon himself, and the wickedness of the wicked shall be upon himself.'"

"I haven't mentioned not visiting the sins of the father upon the child, or grandchild, no," Nicole said. "I'm not sure how he would take that. We're not that religious, you see."

"That's all right. He might also hear it as a good argument. He is a lawyer, isn't he?" Rachel asked.

"He is," Nicole said. "That's true. He might listen if he were hearing it as an argument in a case. Oh, but I hate that I have to present a case to my husband! Why does it have to be an argument at all?"

"I hate to tell you, dear, but that is what a lot of marriage is about. Arguments, and compromise to resolve those arguments."

"But I hate fighting," Nicole said.

"An argument doesn't have to be a fight," Rachel said. "You can disagree about something without having to fight or turn it into something unpleasant. You are two different people with two different sets of needs and desires. It makes sense that you will not agree all the time! I think this is a silly modern notion that husbands and wives will always agree with one another because they are so in love. Please! The true sign of being so in love is being willing to have a difficult conversation with your spouse so that you can reach a place you are both okay with, even if neither of you is entirely happy with it."

"Well, that does sound very wise, Rachel, but—and I mean this with all respect—what compromise can there possibly be between 'I want to start a family now' and 'I do not want to start a family'?" Nicole set her teacup on the table next to her more forcefully than she intended, and she heard how her voice was rising. She simply was not capable of talking about this subject without getting upset.

Rachel carried on with her knitting, bringing row after row of bright-green wool into a shape that would soon be recognizable as the back of a sweater.

"You have already solved one of the big problems—to have children or not to have children. So now it is a matter of timing. That is a much smaller problem to have. I realize it doesn't feel that way, but it really is better. You do not want to convince a man to be a father. Aaron wants to have children, yes?" Nicole nodded. "And you two have been married for three years?" Nicole nodded again. "And when did the disagreement take place between your fathers?"

"Nearly three years ago," Nicole said. "Pretty soon after our wedding."

"All right, so for two and a half years, he has said he will not have children yet. Perhaps you can talk with him about setting up a timeline so that you are not in this limbo place. That seems to me to be why you are so unhappy—because you don't know if this ban on having babies will last for another month or another five years. Does that sound right?"

"Yes. Oh, Rachel, you really get it. I hadn't been able to articulate it to myself, but yes, that is what is so hard for me. I want a baby now, but if I knew we would try in another year or maybe even two, I could be patient. But I can't be patient for five years. I just can't.

And what if too much time goes by, and he doesn't even want a baby with me anymore?"

"That seems like a reasonable thing to say to Aaron," Rachel advised.

"Yes, I can do that," Nicole agreed. "This is good. I've been wanting to act on this for several weeks now, but I wasn't sure where to begin. It seems like we just talk in circles whenever we talk about the topic of babies, but I think now we can have a real discussion about it."

"I'm glad to hear it," Rachel said. She held up her knitting and cast a critical eye over it. "I think this will do. What do you think? For my youngest grandchild."

The green wool looked soft in the light, and the knitting was tight and even. Looking at it, Nicole didn't see an object she was envious of like she usually was when she saw baby clothes for other women's babies. Instead, she saw a well-made gift from a loving grandmother to her grandchild, and she felt generous enough to say so.

"It looks lovely," Nicole said. "She'll love it." Rachel smiled.

———

That evening, Nicole made meat loaf, Aaron's favorite, and opened a good bottle of wine. She put candles on the table and used their wedding china.

When Aaron walked in the door, he took an exaggerated deep breath and said, "Wow, that smell! Are you making meat loaf?"

Nicole smiled and kissed him hello.

"Sit down; it's ready," she said.

"My timing is perfect," Aaron said, taking off his suit jacket and loosening his tie. "What's the occasion?"

"No occasion," Nicole said. "It's been a while since I made it, and you like it so much."

"You make it so well. Burnt at the edges. Almost as well as my mom," Aaron teased.

Nicole rolled her eyes but smiled. They dug into the meal and ate in companionable silence for a few minutes.

Then Nicole took a swallow of wine for courage and said, "Actually, I also made it so you would be in a good mood, because I want to bring up a difficult subject."

Aaron slowly put his fork down and sat back in his chair.

"Okay, go ahead," he said.

"I want to talk about having children," Nicole said. Aaron raised his eyebrows. "I know we have discussed it before, but I feel like we only talk in circles, and we both come out of it feeling frustrated."

"That's true," Aaron agreed.

"I was talking with a friend today, and she reminded me that what we have now is not a true compromise, and that great marriages are built on compromise. Right now, we have your ultimatum that we won't have children for an unspecified time because you are rightfully angry with my father."

"I suppose that is how we left it, yes," Aaron said, reaching for his wineglass and taking a drink.

"What I'm asking for," Nicole said, plowing ahead though she was trembling inside, "is for a timeline. I don't like being in this kind of limbo, not knowing if or when I get to start planning a family. I accept that you still need more time to forgive my father, but I'm hoping that since he apologized to you, you would be able to come to forgiveness more quickly."

"Yes, I've been trying to bring myself to forgiveness more actively since he and I had that talk. It's difficult because I haven't talked to my own father about it yet. I'm not sure what to say, and I don't know if it would upset him, so I haven't brought it up."

"I can understand that," Nicole said, reaching out to put a hand on his. Aaron put his other hand on top of hers, and they sat for a moment in silence, feeling all the emotions that this topic brought up in both of them.

"All right," Aaron said suddenly. "You're right, I can't keep you in suspense for forever. Can I have another few months, maybe up to a year, and then we will start trying?"

Nicole shrieked with joy. "Yes! Oh, Aaron, that is wonderful. Thank you."

Aaron grinned and stood, pulling Nicole out of her seat and into a close embrace.

"I'm sorry to have kept you waiting this long," he murmured into her ear. "That was selfish of me. You know I want to have a child with you."

"I'm so glad to hear you say it. I know that you did once upon a time, but I was starting to think you didn't want to anymore," Nicole whispered back. Aaron squeezed her tightly.

"Never. We are going to have beautiful children," he said.

"We certainly are," Nicole said.

Aaron released her from the hug and held her out at arm's length, looking her up and down in appreciation. "Let's finish up this wine. We might not be making a baby tonight, but I want to practice."

Nicole laughed and picked up the wine bottle. "I'm right there with you."

CHAPTER THIRTY-FIVE

Jacob couldn't remember the last time he had been in a classroom situation. Law school, he supposed. That seemed a lifetime ago. He and Gail had been just starting out, and he'd been so full of ambition—ready to prove to everyone that he was just as good, if not better, than all of them. Looking back, he realized that for all his talk of being a self-made man, he couldn't have done it on his own. Gail kept him fed and clothed so he could focus on his studies, and her job as a secretary paid for their modest lifestyle while he was racking up law school debt. Michael got him his first real job when he started practicing. And it seemed increasingly possible that "someone up there" had been looking out for him too.

Gail leaned over and said, "Here he comes," and Jacob shook himself out of his reverie as Rabbi Eisel walked onto the bimah.

"Welcome to this evening's class on one of the most famous passages from the Torah, Proverbs 6:16," the rabbi began. "You probably know them as the seven deadly sins." Behind Rabbi Eisel, a pull-down screen displayed the sins: lust, gluttony, greed, sloth, wrath, envy, and pride. Jacob started matching up his own actions to the sins and was ashamed to find how many examples of each were in his life.

"The number seven is special to God," Rabbi Eisel continued. "It took seven days to create the world, and God rested on the seventh day. Therefore, the number seven is a one of completion and perfection. King Solomon, said to be the wisest man to ever live, discussed the seven deadly sins in the Book of Proverbs. But for Jews, when a Jew commits a sin or a transgression, he still has the possibility to repent, and to correct his actions and be forgiven by men and by God. As such, for every sin, there is a virtue."

He clicked his pointer, and the screen now displayed the sins and their corresponding virtues: lust/chastity, gluttony/temperance, greed/charity, sloth/diligence, wrath/patience, envy/kindness, and pride/humility.

"One who has sinned should identify what kind of sin it was, and then endeavor to perform a virtuous act to counter it. For example, one who has sinned by displaying envy can perform acts of kindness. One who is guilty of wrath can exercise patience."

Jacob started thinking about how he could make these amends in his life. Donna had worked for him for over twenty years, and he was only ever envious of her ease with people instead of celebrating it. He could get her flowers. And the next time he went to visit Dr. Lowy, he would fill out the forms as requested and make small talk with Cindy the receptionist, rather than show impatience.

Rabbi Eisel carried on: "And the Talmud says that to give of yourself by performing acts of charity is the most powerful force in the world. So great that it can even save one from death!"

Jacob saw Gail looking at him out of the corner of her eye. She must be thinking the same thing he was: she had told him she didn't want to be the richest person in the cemetery. Well, from now on, they would make sure they weren't. He would pick up pro bono work. He would give money to people begging, like that man on the freeway off-ramp. He would give food to homeless shelters. What's more, he would personally contribute funds to Mr. Woo's mother's recovery, and he would write the letter that Mr. Woo had asked for. Just a letter, such a simple thing. Why had he thought himself above it?

"One who has committed the sin of lust, even just in the mind, must practice chastity," Rabbi Eisel said.

This time, Gail peered directly at Jacob. He bowed his head and squeezed her hand. Yes, he would have to put an end to Claire Harris's calls permanently. It wouldn't be a pleasant conversation; he had been leading her to believe that they would move into a physical relationship, and despite what he had told Donna and Gail, he hadn't told Ms. Harris to stop her flirtatious calls. He would have to do that, and he was sorry to have to hurt her feelings. He never should have allowed the flirtation in the first place. If he had practiced more chastity from the start, neither Claire Harris nor Gail would be hurt now. And all because Jacob liked the ego boost.

He massaged the back of his neck. This was a tough class.

Rabbi Eisel was wrapping up. "It is difficult to ask for forgiveness. But it is impossible to free oneself of the ballast of one's negative actions unless one has asked for forgiveness from the one that was hurt. Once you ask for and are granted forgiveness, it is a great relief. And the trauma of having to humble yourself and ask for forgiveness will help assure that you think twice before hurting someone again. It is also one of the greatest mitzvahs."

Jacob didn't need to see Gail's face or look at the screen to know that he had to ask forgiveness for committing sins of greed and pride, and he had to ask it of the person he had wronged most grievously.

It was time to visit Michael.

CHAPTER THIRTY-SIX

It felt strange, being back in the old office. Jacob hadn't set foot there in two years. He liked the fresh flowers Michael's secretary, Jane, always had on her desk, and the way the south-facing windows let in the light. There seemed to be a new piece of art on the wall, some sort of landscape. Jacob leaned forward to get a closer look, but just then Jane finished her phone call and said his name.

"Hi, Jane," Jacob replied, turning and walking over to her desk.

"Mr. Abrams, I heard you had, uh . . ." She struggled to find the right words.

"Yeah, I had a heart attack," Jacob confirmed. "I guess word spreads quickly. But I am doing better. Ah, look, Jane, I know I don't have an appointment, but I was wondering if Michael could see me. It will take just a moment."

"He is quite busy, but let me try," Jane said. She picked up her phone and buzzed Michael while Jacob shuffled his feet nervously.

"Michael, Mr. Abrams is here and he—"

"Send him back," Michael said briskly over the intercom. Jane smiled up at Jacob and waved him through to the back.

"Thanks, Jane," Jacob said, heading down the hall. When he reached Michael's office door, he took a deep breath, then went in.

Michael's office was laid out much like Jacob's, but his office was neat and tidy, with all the client files stacked on a corner of his desk. Where Jacob "decorated" his office with cigarette smoke, Michael had placed a few plants near the window, and framed photos of his family took pride of place on a shelf directly behind his desk so visitors could see them. Jacob was pretty sure he had a photo of Gail and Nicole somewhere under his piles of files. He would have to unearth it when he returned to work.

"Sit down," Michael said in the generous manner of someone who knows they have the upper hand. Jacob sat.

"That's a beautiful picture of the kids," Jacob offered, pointing to one of Nicole and Aaron at their wedding.

"Thanks," Michael said, turning his head slightly to look at the photo, and smiling at the memory of that day. "But I am sure you are not here to admire my photos."

"Ah, no," Jacob said. He couldn't seem to go on. His tongue felt too large in his mouth. Rabbi Eisel was not kidding about how hard it was to ask for forgiveness.

"You almost died," Michael said.

"I did."

"And now?"

"I am changing my ways," Jacob promised, feeling like he'd landed in a cross-examination with no preparation.

"It's not like you didn't have a warning," Michael observed. "You always ate like shit, drank too much, and wouldn't give up the cigarettes . . . Anyway, I'm sure you don't need to hear that from me. What brings you here, Jacob?"

Jacob swallowed and rubbed his hands back and forth on his trouser legs. He was always so in charge, but now, even though he

knew what he wanted to say, he felt intimidated. This must be what
it was like for people on the witness stand.

"Our families have a history; our kids are married, and you and
I go back many years," Jacob said. "I want that history to continue.
What I did was wrong. And I am here to apologize. You have been a
great friend to me for so much of my life, Michael, and I miss you."

Michael leaned back in his chair and stared at Jacob for what felt
like a year. Finally, he spoke, but to Jacob's surprise, it wasn't a direct
answer to what he'd just said.

"Do you remember how we met?" Michael asked.

"Of course. You were renting space from old man Greenbaum,
and he had an extra office because someone moved out."

"Yeah, and I called you. You were at the DA's office and hated it.
You wanted to go on your own, and you seemed like someone I could
work with. You know, Greenbaum is still alive."

"Really?" Jacob replied, his eyebrows shooting up. He'd been old
twenty years ago.

"His wife died a few years back, and he now lives in a board of
care not far from here," Michael said.

"He never had kids," Jacob remembered.

"No, he is all alone. Diane and I visit him," Michael said. "His
body is weak, but his mind is still sharp. He enjoys our visits. But
you wouldn't know about doing good deeds."

Jacob opened his mouth to counter that, actually, he was
embarking on a new life of good deeds, but Michael continued.

"Remember that first case I referred you? The family had no
money. But I said take it as it would pay you rewards in the future.
And it did. You were their hero, and you had so many referrals you
almost couldn't keep up."

Jacob nodded. He could still see them in his mind, gratitude
radiating from their faces. He'd been so proud of that case—because
he had won, he always assumed, but maybe some of his pride came
from knowing he'd helped people who needed it.

Michael leaned forward in his chair and raised his voice slightly. "I was a loyal partner and your friend. Every penny I took in, I accounted for. Because I thought you would do the same. But when I had the opportunity to get appointed to the bench, you decided that I would screw you on our open cases. How you could possibly think that of me, I don't know. So, you aligned yourself with that ambulance chaser, Weiner."

"He pronounces it 'Wee-ner,'" Jacob couldn't help pointing out.

"Who gives a fuck," Michael almost shouted. "How did he ever pass the bar? And not only that, but you started siphoning off cases. How did you think I wouldn't find out? We're a small office. What were you thinking?"

"I don't know. I don't have a good reason for any of it," Jacob said in a small voice.

"I'll tell you why. You did it all for greed," Michael pronounced. "Well, guess what, Jacob. You can take your gated home and your big fancy car and your boat and your expensive wines. Take your Lakers seats behind Jack. Just remember that when they bury you, the only thing they throw in the hole is your casket. And I hope you spend all of your money on medication!" Michael was red in the face. He paused and pushed his graying hair back distractedly. "I'm sorry. That was hitting below the belt."

"I deserve it," Jacob said. "I deserve everything you've said. All those things I did were wrong, and I am so, so sorry. You were a good partner and a good friend, and I didn't treat you accordingly."

Michael looked deep into Jacob's eyes. "You're pathetic," he said quietly.

They sat like that for a moment, Michael looking at him with anger and pity, Jacob forcing himself to stay open to it even though the judgment hurt. Jacob felt just how much he missed Michael, missed him so much he ached. Even when Michael was yelling at him, Jacob missed him. They were like that sometimes when they were working together; Jacob would bring a case by Michael's office, and they would argue over the best way to approach it. Sometimes they even raised their voices, but it was all in their passion for the law and the good-spirited ego jostling of people who knew their friendship could survive a few jibes.

Over twenty years, they'd been close friends and business partners, growing from young men to middle-aged parents together. Jacob really was pathetic, to have thrown that all away on small-minded jealousy and greed. And to have let his pride keep him from apologizing for so long, well, Jacob could hardly stand to think about it. He was glad he'd apologized to Aaron first, as it gave him the courage to come talk to Michael (with the extra boost from the rabbi's class).

Jane buzzed in on the intercom. "Michael, your wife is on the phone."

Michael grabbed the phone. "Diane. You will never believe who is in my office—Jacob Abrams. He came to apologize." Michael looked over at Jacob, who remained motionless, his hands resting in his lap, his eyes downcast. "I didn't give him an answer. Okay. I'll call you in a little bit. Okay, I will."

He hung up the phone and cleared his throat. Jacob looked up tentatively.

"Diane said she hopes you feel better," Michael relayed. "And to say hello to Gail."

"I will," Jacob said.

"Do you know how hurt she is? How uncomfortable it is when she's in the same room as Gail? They were best friends, and now, every time she sees her . . . And did you not think how this would affect Aaron and Nicole?" Michael shook his head. "She hopes you feel better. Women are too forgiving. And if she ever knew everything!" Jacob gulped, unsure if he could hear more of his sins just now. But Michael seemed deflated, as if their conversation had taken it all out of him.

"I need some time," Michael said. "I need to think about this."

"I understand," Jacob said meekly. "Thank you for hearing me out."

"Well, you know I have an open-door policy," Michael said.

"Even for bums like me," Jacob ventured a joke. But Michael just stared at him. Too soon, apparently.

Jacob stood and moved toward the door. When his hand was on the handle, he turned back and said, "I talked with Aaron a couple months ago about this. I have been thinking about how my actions affected Diane and Gail, and Aaron and Nicole also. I'm working my way through apologizing to everyone. I was afraid to come here, I won't lie, Michael. I knew you were the one I had hurt the most deeply, and you are the one I feel most ashamed to come to. But as the rabbi says, asking for forgiveness is one of the greatest mitzvahs."

"The rabbi, huh, Jacob? You were never a religious man."

"Well, I'm taking God's advice into account more, lately," Jacob said with a small smile. Michael stared hard at him for a moment, then nodded.

"Well, good. That can only be to the good," he said.

"I hope so," Jacob said. "Thanks for your time, Michael. I hope we can talk soon."

"I'll let you know if and when I'm ready," Michael replied.

Jacob nodded and let himself out.

CHAPTER THIRTY-SEVEN

Nicole pushed her hair nervously behind her ear and fiddled with the strap on her purse. She had parked in her parents' driveway almost five minutes ago. She was trying to talk herself into going into the house but had not yet worked up the nerve. Finally, she said to herself sternly, "Nicole, you're a big girl. Go in there and have a talk with your father."

She unbuckled the seat belt and opened the car door, got halfway out, remembered the keys, reached back in for them, and then left the car too quickly, bumping her head as she stepped out. "Ouch!" she cried. Obviously, she still had some nerves. She wished she had her running shoes. She would go for a quick jog around the lake behind the house and calm herself down.

Instead, she readjusted her shirt over her nice slacks and closed the car door firmly. She marched up the walk to her parents' house and opened the door.

"Hello, anyone home?" she called. She knew her mother was

out; she had called her earlier to check that she was at her hair appointment as she usually was at this time.

"Nicole, is that you?" she heard her father call from the living room. She headed back there, meeting Riley along the way, who rubbed his face against her as she walked.

"Hi there, Riley. You doing okay?" she asked, bending down to scratch behind his ears.

"He's doing fine. Wishes we gave him more to eat, but then what's new?" Jacob said. She looked up. He stood in the doorway to the living room, looking better than he had in months, the glow of exercise and healthy food emanating from him. She smiled. It was good to see him looking good.

"Hi, Dad," she said, standing and reaching over to kiss his cheek.

"Hi, sweetheart," he replied, giving her a hug. "What a nice surprise. To what do I owe the pleasure?"

"Oh, well, it's been a while since it was just you and me, hasn't it? And I wanted to see my dad. So, I thought I'd come by. I called your office, and Donna said you took a half day. You never do that!"

"Doctor's orders," Jacob said with a grimace. "Lowy says I'm doing better but I need to be careful not to let the stress build back up, because that's a major factor in problems with the ol' ticker," he said, tapping his chest. "So, I'm on half days a couple days a week."

"Now that you say that, I think Mom did mention something to me. How are you finding it?" Nicole asked as they walked into the living room and sat, he on his chair and she on the sofa.

"Dull. Lowy says it doesn't count if I bring the work home with me, so I either watch more *Judge Judy* or take a nap, or sometimes I take longer walks around the lake. But it's all meant to be rest, rest, rest, so I really can't do much more. It's so boring!" he said, slapping his knee, which startled Riley, who leaped out of his lap onto the floor. "Oops, sorry, bud. You can come back if you want to," he said to Riley, but the cat eyed him warily from the window and then turned away to look outside.

"I guess he decided you're an unstable surface for the moment," Nicole said.

"I guess so," Jacob agreed.

"I'm sorry it's so boring, Dad," Nicole said. "Too bad you don't fish or something. I bet Dr. Lowy would let you do that down at the lake."

"That's true," Jacob mused. "I hadn't thought of that. You're such a smart girl. My angel. How are you?"

"I'm all right," Nicole said. "I actually wanted to talk with you about something, but it's a little upsetting, and I'm worried about straining your heart."

"Well, with a lead-in like that, my heart is definitely going pitter-pat now! What's wrong?" Jacob said, sitting straighter in his chair.

"Oh no, I'm okay—nothing wrong like that," Nicole reassured him. She smoothed her skirt and took a deep breath. "The thing is, Dad, I wanted to talk with you about your fight with Michael."

Jacob closed his eyes and heaved a big sigh.

"Oh, I'm sorry, is this a boring topic?" Nicole said sarcastically.

"No no, sweetheart, I was just preparing myself because it's a difficult topic," Jacob said, opening his eyes and leaning forward in his chair.

"Oh, okay," Nicole said, immediately chastened.

"I'm sorry, I interrupted you. Go on," Jacob encouraged her.

"Well, Dad, we got a call last night from Michael. He said you had stopped into his office and apologized—for the judgeship and Weiner, for siphoning off cases, all of it."

"Yes, I did," Jacob confirmed.

"I was so glad to hear it," Nicole continued. "I know Michael is still considering what to do, and I'm sure he and Diane have a lot to discuss. But it was good of you to go there in the first place."

"It was far too little, and too late," Jacob said. "I know that. But it was all I could do. I wish I could go back in time and shake myself out of whatever idiot frame of mind I was in, but I can't."

"And I appreciate that, Dad. I know we can't go back in time. But I realized I never talked with you about what that experience was like for me, and for me and Aaron. I don't know if it's right for me to bring this up when you have already asked for Michael's forgiveness, but it's been weighing on my mind." Nicole looked over at her father. He was gazing at her with such love and sadness.

"Of course you should bring it up, Nicole," Jacob said. "Please tell me whatever you need to tell me. I am ready to hear it."

"Well," Nicole said, taking a deep breath, "I guess one of the things is that I wonder why you apologized to Aaron and Michael but not to me? Why did Aaron get your consideration, but I did not?"

"I should have. I see that now," Jacob said. "I should have come to you on my knees and begged your forgiveness for blighting your first married year with my greed and jealousy. And then when I finally started to realize just how terrible I had been (which is only what your mother has been telling me for two and a half years), I should have come to you first. I don't know why I didn't. I suppose it's because I was so ashamed, I wasn't sure I could. I felt a lot of shame with Aaron, yes, but you are still my daughter, and it seemed that much worse to have failed you. I suppose that's a cowardly reason, but it's the only one I have." He started to weep quietly. Nicole wasn't sure she had ever seen him cry before this past year. His heart problems and recovery program had really opened his emotions in surprising ways.

"Thank you, Dad," she said quietly.

They sat in silence for a moment, while Riley crept onto Nicole's lap and curled up there. Nicole started petting him, taking comfort in his warm, soft fur.

"There is one more thing I wanted to mention, Dad. It almost seems cruel now because I know how sorry you are, but . . ." Nicole trailed off.

Jacob shook his head and managed a weak smile. "That's okay, Nicole. I'm tough. Your old man can take it!"

Nicole gave a shaky smile in return.

"Well, it's just that one of the things that made your actions so difficult to bear was that Aaron and I have delayed starting a family because it was too stressful while our families weren't talking to one another. I know you and Mom really want grandkids, but that won't be possible for at least a little while, while we try to let these wounds heal."

Jacob started crying again. "Oh, my sweetheart, oh no," he said, rocking slightly and holding his hands against his chest.

Nicole jumped up from the sofa, causing Riley to scramble across the room and meow in protest. Nicole rushed over to her dad's chair and knelt next to it.

"Dad, are you okay? Dad!"

"I'm fine, I'm fine. Maybe a glass of water," he mumbled.

Nicole leaped up and ran to the kitchen to get a glass of water. She rushed back with it and knelt again to give it to him. She watched him anxiously as he drank half the glass, then put it down next to him and took both her hands in his.

"My dearest angel, Nicole, I am so deeply sorry to hear that. I ask your forgiveness for the pain I have caused you."

"I forgive you, Dad," Nicole said, finally letting the tears loose.

"Thank you, thank you. I hope that when you and Aaron are ready, you are able to start your family, and it will be a blessing."

"I hope so too," Nicole said through her tears. The two of them held each other for a long time, their heads bowed and their arms around each other. Father and daughter, united in a grief and a hope for a better future.

Gail found them like that when she came home from her hair appointment some minutes later.

"What's going on?" she asked. "And why is Riley hiding under the sofa?"

Nicole and Jacob burst into laughter.

CHAPTER THIRTY-EIGHT

O ver the next several months, Jacob threw himself wholeheartedly into what he called his "body and soul" routine. His conversation with Nicole had really shaken him. If the past few months had shown him anything, they had shown him just how destructive his behavior had been to the others in his life, and yet he had managed to avoid thinking about how that applied to his beloved Nicole. Nicole, who from her very first moments of life had captured Jacob's heart, and whom he had worked so hard to provide a good life for. And now, to find out that all that work was for nothing; or at least it felt that way, if instead of feeling his love and support she had felt betrayed and like she had to change her entire life course—delaying having a child—because of his actions. What kind of man had he been? What kind of man did he still have time to become?

The "body" part of his routine was simple to follow. Not fun, but it was simple. He ate what Gail fed him, he drank what she said he could drink, he slapped on nicotine patches instead of lighting up, and he did a double circuit of the lake behind their house every day. Dr. Lowy assured him the nicotine patches would be almost the same as smoking, but clearly Lowy had never been a smoker, because they were nowhere close. Gail worked to make the food as tasty as possible, and because she was a good cook, it was a lot better than it could have been. She'd improved since that first meal of under-seasoned chicken and limp pasta.

He missed his scotch, although the doc let him have one glass every couple of weeks. Jacob found that he savored that drink as he'd never savored any drink before, and he swore he found new levels of flavor in each precious sip. He spotted the metaphor in that, even before Gail pointed it out, and they had a really good conversation that night about what they were grateful for and how they could show that gratitude to each other and to God.

Jacob did like the walks. That part was not difficult for him to get into. He walked more slowly than he used to, and he felt each twinge in his knee and each pinch in his hips as he strolled along, but he felt energized at the end of the walk, and he enjoyed feeding Laker. He also got into a rhythm when he walked, almost meditative, and he spent a lot of this time reflecting. This was part of his "soul" routine—thinking about his past sins and how he could atone for them and do better in the future, as the rabbi had said. He was working at the food bank, doing pro bono work, and donating money to charities, and he found that once he started, he liked it. Donating to charity was the easiest, since all he had to do was sign a check or agree with what Gail said she was going to give. The food bank work was fun, just as Lowy had promised it would be. He and the other guys had an easy rapport, and he felt good knowing that people were eating better food than they might otherwise be able to get, and all because he stopped by a couple shops and asked for their leftovers.

The pro bono work was the toughest, as it turned out. He'd worked in criminal law for years, but only ever for the guys who could pay, and he was almost always sure that they had actually done the crimes he got them acquitted for. Now he had a couple cases that the overloaded public defender was only too happy to hand over, and this was a whole different ballgame.

These clients were almost all poor, and they were accused of things like petty theft or unlicensed marijuana sales. Some of them could have been in and out of the system in a matter of days, except that their hearings got postponed, or they couldn't make bail, and they languished in jail for weeks, sometimes months, on end. There was so little that Jacob could do for them, and he was humbled to see this side of the justice system, the side that barely creaked along and lost plenty of people in the cracks. Jacob felt a little hopeless when he did this work, but he forged ahead, determined to help, even if it was just a little; and his stubborn nature served him well here, pushing past bureaucratic holdups and underpaid clerks and the whole inefficient, moneymaking mess.

Recently, he'd done a hard afternoon's work getting his client's bail processed before Friday at 5 p.m. so she could be home with her kids for the weekend. She said something in rapid Spanish that he didn't understand, then took him firmly by his shoulders and kissed him on each cheek.

"You're welcome, you're welcome," Jacob said, embarrassed and unsure what to do with his hands. He settled for an awkward pat on the back.

"Thank you, Mr. Abrams," she said again as she walked out the door.

Jacob felt a warm glow in his heart as she left—like the feeling he'd had those many years ago when he took that pro bono case Michael had insisted on. It was pride in a job well done, yes, but also pride in doing a good deed for a fellow human being.

Jacob thought about all this as he made his slow way around the lake. He also considered this second chance he'd been given. He often puzzled over who the stranger with the hidden eyes was. There was no way he was several different people, because he looked the same, but equally there was no way he could be the same one person, following him all over from California to Hawaii and back. It was entirely possible the stranger was a hallucination brought on by stress, of course. Jacob had never interacted with him when other people were around, so no one could confirm or deny his existence.

Another possibility, one that filled Jacob with a dread he could hardly acknowledge, was that he was some sort of spirit. Not that Jacob believed in spirits, not really. He was a rational, educated man, and yes, he believed in God, but this whole business of angels and spirits was more than he could go for. Right?

But if the stranger was some sort of spirit, he certainly didn't feel like a good one. What did that mean for Jacob? The man's appearance obviously portended ill health. Did he also bring doom? Was he a punishment for past sins, and could he be fended off with good deeds now? Jacob was certainly doing his best to test this part of the theory—a theory that he kept to himself, lest Gail or Nicole send him to a different kind of doctor than Lowy, one with a degree in psychiatry.

CHAPTER THIRTY-NINE

The highlight of that period was when Michael called Jacob and said he could forgive him. Jacob was at work, chatting with Donna in the reception area. He had just brought her a coffee, and she was filling him in on her vacation plans. In all the years she'd worked for him, he had never asked her about her personal life, but now he wanted to know where she was going and what she planned to do, and she was happy to show him the hotel website and describe the activities she had booked.

The phone rang, and Donna said, "Excuse me, but if I don't answer this, my boss will be very upset." They both laughed, and Jacob pushed himself off her desk and walked to the door of his office.

"Hello?" Donna said. "Oh, Michael, hello! How are you?"

Jacob froze. His heart started to race, and he gripped the doorpost. He couldn't turn around.

"Just a moment, Michael," said Donna. "Um, Jacob, it's Michael Green on the line. Shall I put him through?"

Jacob pried his fingers loose and forced himself upright.

"Yes, Donna, put him through, thanks," he said in as cheerful a voice as he could muster. He walked into his office and closed the door. The phone buzzed as he sat, and he took a deep breath before answering.

"Michael, hello," he said.

"Jacob, hi." Michael's voice sounded sure and confident over the phone. Jacob wished he could feel the same way. "I'm sorry to bother you during the workday. I know how you hate for personal business to interfere with business."

"Oh no, that's fine. I was just talking with Donna about her vacation, in fact. I've loosened up a lot," Jacob said, trying for a light tone but feeling that he'd missed it.

"Well, that's fine. Look, Jacob, I wanted to call because I've given a lot of thought to what you said when you visited here last week, and I've talked it over with Diane and Aaron, and I've prayed about it. Your apology was sincere, and you seem to really be trying to make amends. I forgive you for what you did to me and our families. I want us to be friends again."

A sob of joy escaped from Jacob. "Michael, thank you! Oh, thank you so much. This means the world to me. I've missed you. You were always the moral compass of our office, and of our friendship. I'll try to be better guided by you now."

"Oh, I'm just as human as you are, Jacob. Maybe a little less hotheaded is all," Michael said generously.

"I won't lie, I've still got a bit of bark to me, but I am happy to say very little bite. Except on my clients' behalf, of course."

"Of course." The two men laughed, and Jacob felt a healing start, three years overdue.

———

Jacob called Gail and told her he'd be coming home early, and asked her to please make his favorite of the healthy dishes, the one with the nice tomato sauce. She said she'd run to the shops. Jacob was reminded again of how sweet his wife was, and he could not wait to get home and tell her that.

When he walked in the door, Gail was stirring the sauce on the stovetop. Jacob walked straight to her and enveloped her in a hug.

"What's this for?" she asked.

"I love you—that's what it's for," he replied.

"That's all right, then. I love you too, Jacob. Now scoot; I have to stir this sauce."

Jacob scooted, taking plates out of the cupboard and setting them on the table as Riley wound through his legs, nearly tripping him up.

They sat down to dinner, and as they dug in, Jacob said, "Thanks for the meal. I wanted a special one, because tonight we're celebrating."

"We are?"

"We are. Michael called me at work. He's decided to forgive me, and he wants to be friends again."

"Jacob! That is wonderful news! Oh, I can hardly believe it. I must call Diane. I must call Nicole!"

"We'll do all that, but let's finish this delicious meal first," Jacob said. Gail started to cry, and Jacob held her hand in his. "I know, Gail, I know. I feel the same way."

———

Earlier that day, as Nicole was walking back to her office from the salad bar (in the sneakers she had changed into at work, not her heels this time), she got a call from Aaron.

"Nicole, good news! My father just called," Aaron said jubilantly.

"Oh?" Nicole said, her heart in her throat.

"He's forgiven your father. If my father can, I can too. Dad's going to call Jacob later today, and he and Mom are going to invite us all to a Shabbat dinner this Friday night."

"That's wonderful, Aaron! I'm so happy," Nicole said, stopping in the middle of the sidewalk as a wave of emotions rushed over her.

"Me too," Aaron said. "In fact, I'm so happy, I want you to take a half day at work. I'm leaving the office right now. Meet me at home and take off all your clothes. We don't need to wait for another few months or a year. Let's make our baby now."

Nicole started running.

CHAPTER FORTY

About six months after his heart attack and car crash, Jacob started to notice he was more out of breath on his walks, and his chest sometimes contracted alarmingly when he was working through files at the office. He didn't say anything to Gail because he knew she would get upset, and he didn't want to say anything to Dr. Lowy because he was afraid that he himself might get upset if Lowy told him bad news. He was pretty sure it wasn't good news, but he chose to ignore it and hope it would go away; he couldn't face any other way of dealing with it right now.

The NBA season started back up again, and Jacob arranged for Michael, Aaron, and Lowy to join him at a game. Gail was worried that it would be too much excitement for him, but she was reassured that Dr. Lowy would be there to keep an eye on him. The day of the game, Jacob left the office a couple hours early and told Donna to leave then, too.

"I can stay and get more work done," Donna offered.

"You can if you want," Jacob said, "but only if you take a couple hours for yourself next week. It is only fair, if I get to play hooky for something fun, that you get to do the same."

Donna smiled at this change in him. She had worked for him for over two decades, and he had never once suggested that she take extra time off.

"All right, if you insist," she agreed.

"That's the spirit," Jacob smiled.

"Enjoy the game."

"I will. It's gonna be a good one—I can feel it!"

When he got home, Jacob pecked Gail on the cheek as she finished loading the dishwasher.

"Hi," she said. "You hungry? I have some of that low-sodium turkey if you want a sandwich." Jacob took a glass from the cabinet and filled it with water from the refrigerator door.

"I'm okay, thanks," he said.

"I just spoke to Nicole," Gail said, excitement in her voice. "She said they have something to tell us. And I think I know what it is!"

Jacob drank his water to cover the wave of emotions overcoming him. Happiness, as he realized what the news probably was. Guilt, as his conversation with Nicole from a few months ago was still seared in his memory. Anxiety, as he worried about how it would go when Nicole told them the news; would she mention to Gail what she'd said to him, about how his actions had prevented this moment from happening earlier?

"They're coming over at four tomorrow. I said we could barbecue," Gail continued.

"That's fine," Jacob said, putting his glass down in the sink. "I'm just going to go for a quick walk before the game."

Gail went to him and put her hand to his forehead.

"Jacob, you don't look good," she said worriedly. "You're pale. Are you feeling all right?"

"Yeah, but maybe I'll talk to Lowy tonight," he said. "I think I am coming down with something."

"Then why don't you rest and not go out?"

"I need the exercise," Jacob reminded her.

"I suppose," she relented, "but don't be gone long."

"All right," he agreed. Jacob stepped out into the early evening.

At the lake, Jacob sat on his usual bench and dug into his jacket pocket for his little packet of seeds. He shook some into the water, and Laker paddled over, quacking happily.

"Hey, Laker," Jacob said. "Are we going to win tonight?" He watched in silence as Laker gobbled up the seeds and swam in a little circle.

"I need to tell you something. Something's not right. I don't know. And I am scared. I haven't told Gail because she gets so worried. But you must promise to let me know how things are if, well . . ." Jacob let out a sigh. "You watch out for Gail, all right, buddy? Every so often, waddle over there and check things out. Make sure she's okay. And that neighbor of ours who likes her so much, keep him away. Shake your wet feathers all over him or something."

Laker quacked and started swimming away.

"I'll take that as agreement," Jacob said, standing up. Time to get ready for the game.

━━━━━━━━

Jacob, Michael, Aaron, and Dr. Lowy made their way down the stairs to their seats, just five rows back from the action. Jack Nicholson himself, standing near his seat, spotted Jacob and called out a hello.

"Jacob, how are you? Long time," Jack rasped. "And Michael, even longer!"

Michael grinned in greeting.

"Jack, good to see you. This is Aaron, Michael's son and my son-in-law. And here's my friend George Lowy."

"Pleasure to meet you boys," Jack said. "So, Jacob, where's that very attractive wife of yours?"

"Boys' night out." Jacob shrugged.

"Well, you boys behave. And tell Gail that Jack says hi," Jack said, waggling his famous eyebrows.

"I will. Enjoy the game," Jacob said.

As they filed into their seats, juggling their hot dogs and drinks, Dr. Lowy teased, "You'd better watch out. If you kick off, I know the first call Jack will make."

"He's not Jewish," Jacob argued.

"Oh, excuse me. Knowing your wife, she'll get him to convert."

Michael and Aaron chuckled. Jacob shooed them away and took a big bite out of his hot dog.

Dr. Lowy spoke to him in a lower tone so the other two couldn't hear. "I don't want to embarrass you, but that is not on your diet," he advised.

"Come on, I've been so good. Give me a break tonight," Jacob pleaded. "And don't tell Gail."

"All right, you get a pass," Dr. Lowy agreed. "But just tonight."

"And, George, I do need to talk to you. Maybe you can fit me in at your office in the next couple days?"

Dr. Lowy immediately looked concerned. "What is it?"

"I'm sure it's nothing. It's just I've been feeling a little run-down lately, and I want to check in that everything's good."

Dr. Lowy picked up Jacob's wrist and started counting beats. "Hmm, your heart rate is sounding okay," he said. "But you do look a bit clammy. It might just be a cold, but it could be something more serious. You're right. You'd better come in so I can check it out more thoroughly. I'm sure I can squeeze you in tomorrow. Call Cindy and set it up with her. She sure likes you now that you've started being nice to her."

"I'm a charming guy, what can I say?" Jacob joked.

"Charming, my—" Aaron started.

"Aaron," Michael said in a warning tone.

"Just when you think you're an adult, your dad stops you from swearing and you realize you're never going to be an adult in your parents' eyes," Aaron said ruefully.

Michael and Jacob laughed, and Dr. Lowy put a sympathetic hand on Aaron's shoulder.

It was a close game, and the four men enjoyed following it with the rest of the enthusiastic crowd. But Jacob couldn't ignore the increasing pain. He felt nauseated and was perspiring quite a bit. He had flashbacks to how he'd felt six months ago, and he didn't like it at all. This was the feeling he'd been having over the past week, too. But he'd been so good, sticking to his body and soul routine. Surely God wasn't going to punish him further?

Midway through the fourth quarter, LeBron made an amazing three-point shot, and the crowd roared to its feet. Everyone, that is, except Jacob, who couldn't move. Dr. Lowy noticed and turned to his friend.

"Jacob, are you all right?"

"Yeah, but I should have listened to you. It must be the dog. I guess my body is rejecting it after going so long without eating crap," Jacob said feebly.

Michael and Aaron looked away from the court. Michael put a hand on Jacob's shoulder.

"You're sweating, and your eyes don't seem right," he said.

"I am not feeling right," Jacob gasped before he fell back, his chest constricting in intense pain. He stared up and saw the scoreboard blur into indistinct lights. Suddenly, on the giant screen, instead of the instant replay of the last basket, a figure with shoulder-length black hair and a cleft chin appeared. Jacob started crying as the stranger stepped off the screen and walked toward him, his hand outstretched. A spirit for sure, or the most convincing hallucination he could imagine.

The announcer's voice floated above Jacob's head. "The Lakers call a time-out with 6:16 remaining in the second half." He closed his eyes and saw the faces of Gail and Nicole. And then his parents appeared, and they came into focus, waving at him. Jacob felt Dr. Lowy loosening his shirt collar, and he thought he heard him yelling instructions while Michael called Jacob's name.

Jacob tried to remember how to breathe while in his mind's eye the stranger approached, and behind him, smiling sadly, was Laura.

CHAPTER FORTY-ONE

Here they were again, in the cold artificial light of the hospital. Nicole had hoped that the next time they were here would be for the birth of their child, but it seemed God had other plans. Jacob was hooked up to machines and sleeping, and Nicole and Gail sat in the uncomfortable chairs near the window. They had rushed over when Aaron called them to say that Jacob had had another attack at the basketball game.

Nicole had been enjoying an evening to herself, looking up baby names and giving herself a manicure. She knew something was wrong before Aaron called her, though. She had felt another one of those sudden jolts, so strong and sudden that she'd smeared her nail polish across three of her fingers.

Hands shaking, she cleaned it up with nail polish remover and cotton balls. She had not consciously put these jolts and her father's health problems together, but she knew something was wrong. When Aaron called just a few minutes later with the news, she had already screwed the lid back on the nail polish and grabbed her keys.

Now Aaron was getting a late dinner in the cafeteria with his parents, and they would be back soon to take a shift watching while Nicole and Gail did the same. Dr. Lowy had talked with the doctors in low, urgent tones and then gone home to his wife. He offered to stay, but Gail pointed out that they were in good hands, and he had his own work to get to the next day, so they could not keep him. He promised to stop by to check in.

Jacob had a private room, and Nicole didn't know if that was because her parents paid more for it or if Jacob's condition was so serious that he needed his own space. She hoped that this was another example of her father's desire to always have the best, and not a sign of how bad things were.

The room was quiet except for the humming of the machines and the consistent blip of the heart monitor. The consistency was comforting. It meant his heart was doing what it was meant to be doing, at least for now. The breathing machine was more troubling, as the mask wheezed up and down on Jacob's face and made him look like one of those old photos of people during World War I wearing gas masks.

Nicole shook her head to clear these dark thoughts and tried to focus on the positive. They were in one of the best hospitals in the city. They had a team of doctors and nurses looking after him. They had stabilized him quickly and expected to be able to discharge him soon, maybe even the next day. All was not yet lost.

But this was his second attack, and didn't they always say that the second one was much worse than the first? He had been following Dr. Lowy's orders to get healthy; she knew he had. He was nearly always with Gail or Nicole or Donna, so it would have been hard for him to sneak alcohol or bad foods. And he never smelled like cigarettes, so he seemed not to be secretly smoking, either. He took his walk faithfully every day. And yet, here he was, in as bad a shape as he'd been with the first one, if not worse. *How is that fair?* Nicole asked God. No answer.

"Nicole," her mother said, startling her out of her reverie.

"Yes, Mom?" she asked.

"What's going on with your hands?" Nicole looked down and saw her half-completed manicure, the deep red on her left hand and her right pinky only.

"Oh, didn't you hear? It's the latest fashion," Nicole said, laughing. Gail laughed with her. It was good to loosen up some of the tension in the room.

"I was painting my nails when Aaron called," she explained.

"I see," Gail said. "I was putting together some shish kebabs for the barbecue tomorrow. I just about managed to throw them back in the fridge before I left, so at least the chicken won't spoil."

"Fast thinking, Mom."

"Just habit, I suppose. Although I certainly don't want to get into the habit of being able to put anything down at a moment's notice because I must rush to the hospital. Two times in one year is far too many."

"Agreed. Do you hear that, Dad?" Nicole said, turning to Jacob, who slept under the hum of the machines. "No more hospital visits, please. Let's keep the drama to a minimum."

Gail laughed again, and Nicole was proud of herself for at least doing that. She knew how to smooth things over, and in times of crisis like this, that was a great skill.

A nurse came in and said that she needed to check some measurements on the machines. Would they mind stepping out for a moment? As they stepped out into the hall, they met Michael, Diane, and Aaron coming back from the cafeteria.

"Everything okay?" Diane asked, squeezing Gail's arm.

"Nothing's changed," Gail replied, resting her head on her friend's shoulder. What a deep relief, to have her friends back for this stressful time.

"No news is good news for now, right?" Michael said a little too jovially.

"I think that's the idea," Nicole agreed. Between the two of them, they could buoy everyone's spirits.

The nurse who had been in the room reemerged and closed the door gently behind her.

"Everything's looking good right now," she said. "Sometimes these checkups can disturb the patient's sleep, so if you just want to give it ten or twenty minutes before going back in there."

They nodded mutely. Michael and Diane flanked Gail, and they sat on the bench in the hall. Aaron put his arm around Nicole's shoulders and kissed her forehead.

"Do you want to go down and get some food, or should I bring some up for you?" Aaron asked.

"I think I want to go get some myself," Nicole replied. "Mom?"

"I'd rather stay here," Gail said.

"We'll keep you company," Diane said.

"I'll come with you, then," Aaron said. "The cafeteria was so good; I can't stay away!" Everyone managed a smile at that.

A few minutes later, Nicole sat in a hard plastic chair and put her plastic-wrapped sandwich and plastic bottle of water in front of her.

"Such a wasteful place," she said to Aaron as he settled into the chair across from her. "Look at all this plastic. All this single-use, throw-me-out stuff."

Aaron was used to Nicole's environmental beliefs, and overall, he agreed with her. But he doubted that was really on her mind right now. Still, a distraction might help.

"Yes, I wonder if they've given any thought to reuseables. Didn't you say there was something made of corn?"

"Yes, there's a product made of corn that acts like Styrofoam. It's so much better! And why does my sandwich need to be wrapped like this? Are they so worried about germs? I guess they might be, in a hospital," she said glumly.

"Probably better safe than sorry," Aaron agreed.

"I didn't want to come here for another six months or so," Nicole said.

"Well, we'll still come then, and it'll be a very different mood," Aaron said.

"True," Nicole said, with a brief smile. "I just hope my dad is here to celebrate with us."

Aaron reached across the table and squeezed her hand in his. "He will be; I'm sure of it. Jacob Abrams is a tough guy. It's hard to bring him down."

"But two heart attacks just might do it," Nicole countered.

"Maybe, but the doctors are doing everything they can, and we can't ask for more than that."

"Maybe not. I'm still asking God to spare him, though. It's all I can do, and I need to do something."

"I know how you feel. Your dad will appreciate it."

"I don't know. He's not very religious," Nicole said.

"No, but he seems to be getting more spiritual lately. Haven't you noticed he talks about sin and redemption more? And he is doing all these good deeds," Aaron said.

"That's true. I've been so focused on my own problems and on Dad's physical problems, I hadn't really paid attention to what he's doing on the inside."

"Well, I think he's working hard to find peace with God."

Nicole cried out.

"No, not like that!" Aaron said quickly. "I just mean, I think he's building that relationship with God that you're working on as well. I'm sorry. That was bad phrasing."

"Could've chosen better, Green," Nicole agreed, reverting to calling him by his last name, as she did whenever she was teasing him—as she had done so often when they were children.

"Blame it on the late hour. Blame it on this cafeteria food," Aaron said. Nicole looked down at her half-eaten sandwich and grimaced.

"You should still eat it though, hon. You'll need the strength."

"Fine. I hate it when you're right," Nicole said, picking up the sandwich and taking a big bite just as Michael walked up to them.

"They're going to release him tomorrow. They said to go home tonight; there's nothing more to do here."

Nicole stood quickly, abandoning what was left of the sandwich. "Let's go say goodbye to our moms," she said.

"Right there with you," Aaron replied.

CHAPTER FORTY-TWO
Six months later

It was a quiet evening in Jacob and Gail's house. They sat at the table, eating dinner. The salt and pepper shakers had been replaced by a sea of prescription bottles. A space in the corner had been cleared for Jacob's portable oxygen tank. The calendar was filled with follow-up appointments and medicine refill reminders.

Riley jumped up onto the seat next to Jacob and meowed, but Jacob didn't reach over to pet his head. He'd lost so much weight that his flesh sagged on his large frame, and he sat in a permanent hunch nowadays. Everything seemed like too much of an effort, from walking to breathing, and what was the point of it all? He was on the heart transplant list, but he was sure he wasn't going to get one. He was going to die soon, and the only comfort he had was that Gail was taken care of financially, and Nicole's pregnancy seemed to be going well.

"You're awfully quiet," said Gail, interrupting his sad reverie.

"Oh, I'm sorry," Jacob said caustically. "Were you expecting me to do five minutes of stand-up?"

"You don't have to be obnoxious," Gail said. Jacob didn't respond but stabbed a green bean with his fork.

"I know you are depressed, and I understand," Gail said. "But George said we could get a call any day."

"I don't think so. I don't think I convinced God that I'm deserving," Jacob said morosely.

"I would hope that all the good you did was because you wanted to and not because you thought you needed to," Gail said.

"No, I would still do it," Jacob said, and somewhere inside the fog of hopelessness that engulfed him, he was pleased to note that this was true. He had changed, at least a little. He had seen the good in helping others and not just thinking of himself all the time. "It just seems that whatever I do or touch . . . " He trailed off and started to weep.

"What's wrong?" Gail asked, alarmed.

"I got a call today from Donna. Mr. Woo came by the office. His mother died." Jacob put his head in his hands and continued to weep. "It's my fault."

"Jacob, that's not fair," Gail said, reaching out to touch his arm.

"No, it is," he insisted. "I should have tried to help when he asked for it. But I had already taken his money, and if I couldn't make another buck, I passed. Selfish, greedy, just full of myself. Talking about being a self-made man, but what did I make myself into? I am a bad person and God knows it. All this volunteering and helping— God saw through it all. He knows I am a phony."

"And are you?"

"No! Or at least I don't think so." Suddenly it seemed terribly important that he explain to Gail. "Gail, I've tried so hard. I did not do these good deeds just for form. I started out that way, but after a while I was doing them because it felt genuinely good to do them. I've been, well, I've been thinking about God a lot since the car crash, and especially since you and I went to the rabbi's class."

"Jacob, how wonderful. I'm so proud of you."

"But I also hoped that doing this would help change God's mind about me, that he wouldn't need to punish me anymore for the bad person I used to be. Do you think that hoping for that is itself bad?"

"We seem to be getting into lawyerly territory here, talking about intent and things," Gail said, trying to lighten things a little.

"Ha, maybe," Jacob said. "Once a lawyer, always a lawyer."

"But in all seriousness, Jacob," Gail continued, "I think you know the answer to that. We should do good things because they are good and that is how God wants us to treat one another. But I can't see how it could be sinful to hope that these actions would stand you in good stead with God."

"I hope you're right," Jacob said softly. "I don't want to be hurting my cause just by thinking about it. Oh, I don't know. Anyway, what does any of it matter? We both know I'm not going to . . ." Jacob raised his head from his hands and cleared his throat. "I've been thinking. We need to sell the boat."

"Jacob, no," Gail said, shocked.

"Why so surprised? Since I had the first attack, we've used it once. It's just floating in the slip. And you're going to sell it anyway after I'm . . ." Gail started to cry. "So, I'll make some calls."

"You love that boat," Gail said through her tears.

"While we're on the topic," Jacob said, "that neighbor of ours, the one who always makes time to chat with you over the fence. What's his name?"

"Mr. Williams," Gail said, confused.

"Yeah, he called today while you were out. He was surprised to hear my voice. I guess he thought by now—"

"Stop it," Gail begged.

Jacob pressed ahead, hating that he was hurting her but feeling like he had no choice. These things had to be sorted out before he was gone. And he knew that could be any day now.

"Has Nicole mentioned any names for the baby?" he asked.

"Not that she is saying," Gail said, blowing her nose.

"I don't want them to feel obligated to name the baby after me."

"What?"

"Well, we do name after the dead," Jacob said as gently as he could. Gail started crying again.

"I can't do this, Jacob."

"Earlier, I was in the den, staring out the window," Jacob said. "My mind was playing games with me. I imagined our grandson's first birthday. Aaron was grilling at the barbecue. You were laughing about something with Michael and Diane. It was so real. I could practically smell the hot dogs. But"—and here his voice faltered—"but I wasn't there."

Both Jacob and Gail were crying now, and Riley looked back and forth between them, mewing his concern.

"I want to be there," Jacob said.

CHAPTER FORTY-THREE

Gail sat in Rabbi Eisel's study, the last one in her family to seek guidance from the spiritual leader. Nicole had told her about her visit with him and her own exploration of her relationship with God, and of course Gail knew Jacob had come here and learned about the seven deadly sins class. Maybe Gail should have come sooner, but she'd thought she had everything under control. Now Jacob had had another attack, and he was in a worse depression than before, scaring her with all his talk of dying. She could not think about that. They had just started to feel like a real husband and wife again. They were rediscovering their love for one another. She could not bear to think about that being taken away.

"Gail," the rabbi said warmly. "Thank you for coming by. Can I make you a coffee?"

"Yes, please," Gail replied. "Just a little milk, if you have it."

"Of course. Look at this fancy coffee maker! A generous donation from the Feinbergs. I would have spent the money on something else, but they gave me the actual machine, so I have kept it. Perhaps it was a hint from them on the quality of my coffee before." He chuckled, and Gail managed a strained smile.

The rabbi handed Gail her coffee and took his own in both hands. He leaned back in his chair and looked at Gail with his dark, kind eyes. Gail took a sip of her coffee, found it a bit too hot, and placed the mug on the desk in front of her.

"How is Jacob?" the rabbi asked.

"He is . . . he is . . . oh, he's terrible!" Gail burst into a sob. "He's so much more depressed than he was even after the first heart attack. Then at least he thought he could recover. Now he thinks there is no chance. He's on the heart transplant list, and Dr. Lowy and the specialist have done what they can to get him as near the top of that list as he can be. I make sure he takes all his medication at exactly the right time every day, and I make all the heart-healthy meals from the cookbooks the specialist recommended. He does not exercise anymore, and he is not allowed to work so he doesn't put more stress on his heart. We're doing everything we can, but he is sure that it isn't enough, and that he will, he will"—Gail sobbed again—"that he will die! And I'm worried he might be right."

She subsided into quieter tears. The rabbi looked at her with such compassion that she cried a little more. He pushed a box of tissues across the desk to her, and she gratefully took several. She blew her nose delicately and dabbed at her eyes, careful not to disturb her makeup. She might be on the verge of some sort of breakdown, but she was still Gail Abrams, and she took care of her appearance.

"I am sorry to hear that," the rabbi said. "That's a lot for you both to be going through right now. Jacob is lucky to have you by his side during this time. You are a devoted wife and mother, and it shows."

Gail burst into tears again.

"Gail?"

"Rabbi, I have not felt like a very devoted wife in the last few years. I have . . . well, I have felt and done some things I am not proud of."

"Would you like to talk with me about that?" he offered.

She took a deep breath, then another. "I'm sure you know about the rift between Jacob and Michael Green," she began.

The rabbi inclined his head in acknowledgment.

"Jacob finally apologized a few months ago, and Michael forgave him. We have Michael and Diane back in our lives now, and I am so happy. Nicole and Aaron feel like they can really have a full marriage now that their parents aren't fighting anymore. It's just what I've been hoping for."

"That is very good news."

"Yes, but the time before that was incredibly difficult. Jacob didn't tell me he was going to oppose Michael's bid for judge, so it was a shock to me. One day, I was best friends with the parents of my son-in-law, and the next day, they were out of my life. Poof. Like some horrible magic trick. I was angry with Jacob, Rabbi, and so confused. I wanted to know what had happened. But we never talked about it. He did not want to hear it when I tried to ask him what had happened. He did not want to hear it when I asked him why he needed to set up his own practice."

"You felt cut out of decisions and cut off from your friends?"

"Yes, exactly! One day, I realized that it was more likely that Jacob had just acted out of greed and selfishness, and not out of any actual disagreement he had with Michael. Something snapped in me then. I became so angry, but I didn't know what to do with it. I should have come to you, I think."

"I would have been happy to talk with you then," the rabbi said, "but we are talking now."

"I started shopping. Not like normal. I went into the fancy stores that I usually only visit a couple times a year, and I bought multiple things every time. Clothes, shoes, jewelry. All designer labels. One time I even bought this handmade hat. I don't wear hats! I was never going to wear that hat. I have never worn any of the things I bought in these shopping sprees. I keep them in the back of my closet, where Jacob never goes, so he has no idea."

"Why don't you wear the clothes?" the rabbi asked gently.

"I am ashamed to," Gail said quietly. "I know I should not have bought them. They are an extravagance. I bought them in anger. They are not things I could wear and feel proud. Also, I kept them a secret from Jacob. That's another reason I feel like I've been a bad wife. Now I don't know what to do. I don't want to add to his pain, but I feel so bad about what I have done."

Gail realized she was rubbing her engagement ring hard enough to press the ring painfully into her finger. She held her hand still. Slowly, she met the rabbi's eyes.

"I can see what you mean," the rabbi said. "However, as I am sure you remember from my seven deadly sins class, forgiveness is one of the greatest mitzvahs. You must seek it in order to have a truly honest relationship. If you want to rebuild your relationship with Jacob, you must be honest with him, and he with you. You must ask each other's forgiveness if you are going to be able to move on as husband and wife."

"But what about his heart?"

"I know a shock could be bad for him, but I think you can say it in such a way as to not cause him any physical harm. You are not telling him about an affair, for example."

"You're right. I will do it."

"May I ask if the shopping habit has continued?"

"It hasn't," Gail said quickly. "I found that the urge left me a little while after his first heart attack. I did not get the same thrill from doing it, and I wasn't feeling the same anger that drove me to do it either."

"That's good news," the rabbi said.

"Yes, I was relieved."

"I imagine channeling some of your energy into caretaking helped," the rabbi suggested.

"Yes," Gail agreed, "and he apologized to Aaron and later to Michael, so I was not as angry as I had been before."

"Forgiveness goes two ways," the rabbi observed.

"I hope that's true when I tell him about the shopping sprees," Gail said.

The rabbi set his coffee mug on the desk and laced his fingers together.

"You say that Jacob is feeling like he's going to die soon, even though he is on the transplant list," he said. Gail nodded. "It sounds like he is feeling hopeless, which is a dangerous way to be. I would like to help if I may."

"Please do, Rabbi."

"I think I have an idea, but I will need to make a few calls first. May I get in touch when I have done so?"

"Certainly. Thank you so much, Rabbi," Gail said.

"I am happy to, Gail. I will continue to pray for your family."

CHAPTER FORTY-FOUR

Nicole had a difficult morning, sorting out a thorny client issue that involved talking to three of her colleagues, her manager, and the client's lawyer. She felt a headache coming on, and what's more, she had forgotten to change into her sneakers for the walk to get a salad, and her feet were killing her. She just wanted to get her food and get out of there so she could go back to the office and try to catch up on the work she'd had to let languish while she worked on this client's problem.

The worker scooped up her pinto beans and shook the spoon, started to empty the spoon into the bowl containing her half-made salad, then changed his mind, went back to the pinto bean bowl, and tipped out three, four, five beans back into the bowl.

Nicole lost it.

"What, you're five beans over and that's going to kill you? You think I haven't been waiting long enough for you to make my damn salad, so you're going to drag it out even more? Just put the beans in the salad and move it along!"

The worker flushed red and cast his eyes down, but not before she saw tears start to form there.

"I'm sorry," he said. "We're supposed to be careful to only give exact servings, and I'm trying to get it right. I can get you some more beans."

"No, that will just take longer!" Nicole snapped.

"Right, okay, sorry," he said, and he dumped the beans in her bowl, but in his haste, he knocked the edge of the bowl with the spoon, and the whole bowl tipped over onto the salad bar and all over the floor.

Nicole stared. He stared.

Nicole was filled with remorse. This kid was just trying to do his job, and she'd been mean to him and upset him so much that he'd dropped her meal. He looked like he was trying not to cry. What had she done?

"I'm so sorry," he said.

"I'm so sorry," she said at the same time.

"What? I ruined your salad. I didn't mean to. I'll get you another one, just a minute, I—" he was babbling.

"Wait, wait, wait. It's okay. Please stop. Just wait. I got you all flustered and made you mess up. It's my fault," Nicole said.

"No, if I'd done it right the first time—"

"I shouldn't have made your first time so difficult. But since I did, what do you say we both get a second chance? You make me another bowl, and I'll pay for another one rather than you replace this. I'm sure that comes out of your paycheck, and I couldn't do that."

He looked up gratefully. "Are you sure? I'll try to do it really fast this time," he promised.

"You take the time you need to take," Nicole said. "I won't complain again."

Now, as Nicole sat on her chair and munched on a carrot, she couldn't believe she'd responded like that. Was it pregnancy hormones? Maybe. What it really reminded her of was her father, when he was on one of his tears. He especially loved to take out his frustration on whatever poor customer service person was stuck with him that day. Nicole had seen it more times than she could count, as she grew up. She couldn't say why that had never been her own MO. It would have been easy to emulate her father. But somehow, she never had.

She remembered when she was a teenager, out to dinner with her parents, and her dad had lit into their server for bringing out their appetizer at the same time as the food.

"What do you think it's called an appetizer for, huh, genius? It's supposed to raise my appetite. It's not supposed to be an extra entree. Who trained you? Did they just pick you up off the street, give you a white shirt and black pants, and say, 'Go ahead'? Because you have the intelligence of this tomato here."

"Jacob," Gail said plaintively. "Please."

"Please what? Please don't point out when someone is a total idiot? I'm paying good money for this, good money that I worked hard to earn, at a job that I'm good at. And now some pip-squeak who couldn't even get into college, let alone law school, is going to ruin my evening by bringing me my bruschetta at the same time as my pasta?"

Gail sighed and said, "I'm sorry, young man" to the server, who looked like he wanted to drop dead right there.

Nicole had been sitting quietly this whole time, but she couldn't stand it any longer. She stood and grabbed her purse from the back of her seat.

"Where are you going, young lady?" Jacob said.

"I'm leaving. I don't need to stay here and watch you waste someone just because you're in a bad mood. You're always in a bad mood. I'm the teenager; I'm the one who is supposed to have moods, but you're the one who's always angry. I'm so over it," Nicole said.

"Nicole," her mother tried.

"No, Mom, I don't have to sit here and listen to him have a tantrum. You don't either if you want to come too."

"And just how are you getting home?" Jacob asked.

"I'll ask the hostess to call me a cab. I have cash," Nicole replied.

She'd done it. She left the restaurant and took a cab home. Her parents were furious, and her dad gave her a long lecture on respecting her parents when they got home, but he wasn't as bad with waiters in the future when she was around. He had learned to curb his behavior, even if it took another ten years for him to change it completely.

So, she had never behaved that way to people. That was why it was so upsetting to find herself flying off the handle today at that poor salad bar worker. That didn't feel like something she would do; she hadn't thought it was in her nature.

But what was in nature and what was in nurture? It was a never-ending debate, of course, and she was reading more and more about it in her pregnancy and baby books. Maybe being around that kind of behavior for her whole childhood seeped into her anyway and made her more likely to become someone who lashed out. Maybe it was in her nature, and she'd just been suppressing it this whole time. *What a scary thought, that you can go your whole life thinking you know who you are, and then find at nearly age twenty-seven that you might have a whole other side to you.* It was practically Jekyll and Hyde over here.

Nicole picked up her phone and found Rachel in her contacts, listed as "Rachel Women's Club." The older woman picked up after the third ring.

"Nicole, what a nice surprise. How are you doing? How's the pregnancy?" she said.

"The pregnancy is okay. Thanks, Rachel. Some back pain, but I'm just using that as an excuse to have Aaron do more around the house," Nicole joked. They both laughed. "Um, Rachel, this is a bit awkward, but I was hoping I could ask you for advice. You've been so helpful to me before."

"That's not a problem, dear," Rachel replied. "I just hope I can help."

"Today I did something totally out of character for me. I completely lost it on a food service worker, and almost made him cry. I was super apologetic and paid double for everything, but I still feel terrible."

"Oh my, that does sound unlike you. Were you under a lot of stress?"

"Yes, more stress than usual, and I hadn't eaten in a while, so my blood sugar was low. But still, that's not a normal reaction for me. It is a normal reaction for my father, or at least it used to be before he had this major change of heart. I'm worried that this is some sort of latent part of my personality—that this is who I am now, or that it will come and go and I won't have any control over it. Or what if it really is in my nature, and it's something I pass on to my baby?" Nicole's voice rose in panic as this last thought occurred to her.

"There there, dear, it's not as bad as that. This kind of impatience and outsized reaction is not something that can be inherited, I don't think. We all have bad days, and we all have times when we behave in ways we find surprising. It doesn't mean that your personality is fundamentally changing," Rachel said soothingly. "Remember, you said that you were under stress and you were hungry. Those aren't good conditions for anyone. In fact, those are the exact kind of conditions your baby is going to be in many times, and how will your baby react? By crying and screaming! If you want a case for nature, that's your case right there. It's natural to respond to those conditions in that way."

"That's true," Nicole agreed. "But I didn't have to be cruel."

"No, and I see why that worries you," Rachel said. "Tell me, what was your reaction when you realized that you'd been cruel? What did you feel?"

"I felt remorse, almost right away," Nicole said.

"I think that's good. I think that means that you saw a wrong you committed, you repented, and you immediately tried to right the wrong. That is all God asks of us. He does not ask us to be perfect. He asks us to do our best for ourselves and for others, and that includes recognizing our wrongs and doing what we can to correct them."

Nicole took a deep breath. She heard Rachel patiently waiting on the other end of the line.

"Thank you, Rachel; that's really helpful. I think I've spent so much of my life trying to be the best at everything that when I realized I wasn't being the best, I freaked out. I worried it meant that now I was the worst. But the world isn't black and white, and I'm not perfect. I'm going to make mistakes, and that's okay."

"Exactly," Rachel said. "It's human nature to sin, and human nature to repent and repair that sin. God knows this about us and asks us to be mindful about it."

After they said good night and hung up, Nicole sat in thought for a long time, a half-eaten carrot stick in her hand. She stared into the distance and thought long and hard about what Rachel had said, about how she had been raised, about the changes in her father in the last year, about the changes in herself. She rubbed her belly absentmindedly the whole time. There was a lot to think about.

CHAPTER FORTY-FIVE

Gail chose her timing carefully. She made the breakfast Jacob hated least out of the heart-healthy book and fixed him a small cup of decaf coffee, then cleaned up in the kitchen while he settled in his favorite chair in the living room and patted his lap for Riley to jump into. Switching off the kitchen lights, Gail took a deep breath and walked into the living room. Jacob was just picking up the remote to turn on the TV. Gail took it from his hands and put it on the coffee table.

"Hey," he protested.

"I'm sorry, Jacob. I'll give it back soon. I just wanted to talk with you first," Gail said.

"Talk about what? You change your mind about Williams next door?" Jacob said grumpily. Gail winced and Jacob mumbled an apology.

"No, I wanted to talk because I need to be honest with you, as you have become more honest with me, so that we can have a strong marriage again."

"What? You're always honest with me. Sometimes too honest, telling me how to behave and all."

"This is different. This is about something that I have been doing that I am not proud of."

"I knew it! That Williams, trying to get in there before I'm even in the ground," Jacob joked, but Gail saw a wariness in his eyes.

"Jacob, please, don't mention Mr. Williams again. He has nothing to do with this, or with us, and it hurts me to hear you joke like that."

"I'm sorry," Jacob said, sounding truly contrite.

"Also, it makes it harder for me to say what I need to say. I have not been unfaithful to you, but I have been dishonest." Gail's mouth felt incredibly dry. She swallowed and pressed on. "Ever since you broke up with Michael, I've been going on secret shopping sprees. I have bought some very expensive things—clothes, shoes, jewelry—and hidden them all."

"That's it? You went shopping? Gail, I work hard to make sure you can do that. You don't have to do it in secret. Plus, we share a credit card, so I could see what you're buying anytime."

"Yes, but you don't make sure the credit card is paid up; I do. I deal with the household finances. You have not looked and noticed anything unusual in the past few years, have you?" Gail challenged him.

"No," Jacob admitted. "I haven't gone looking. How much are we talking?"

"Almost $100,000 over the last three years," Gail said quietly.

"One hundred grand? On things you never wear? Are you kidding me?" Jacob erupted, starting to rise from his chair in surprise and anger.

"Jacob, your heart!" Jacob sat back heavily in the chair, put a hand to his chest, and used his other hand to make calming motions to her.

"I'm all right, I'm all right," he said, and he did seem to be okay—no change in color and only breathing a little hard. Gail was relieved.

"But, Gail, a hundred grand! What were you thinking?"

"I wasn't thinking!" she shouted back, surprising both of them with her vehemence. "I was so angry with you for taking away my best friends, for making married life hard for our daughter, for stranding me and not even telling me why. I didn't even think about it. I just bought designer clothes and put them in the closet. I think I wanted to punish you for isolating me and not even talking to me about it. A strange punishment, I know, since you didn't know about it, but it made me feel better at the time."

"And you did this over three years?"

"Yes, I stopped when you apologized to Aaron. I was not as angry after that, and besides, I was looking after you nearly twenty-four seven."

"So at least one good thing came from that heart attack. Stopped you spending us into the ground," Jacob said. Gail closed her eyes, a pained look on her face.

"I am so sorry for breaking your trust like that, Jacob, and for doing anything that might jeopardize the way we live." She looked at Jacob beseechingly. His face softened into a wry smile.

"I forgive you, Gail—of course I do. As you say, I did not even notice the missing money, so it could not have been jeopardizing our lifestyle too much. I'll make enough money to cover it if I ever get back to work."

"You will get back," Gail said almost automatically, reassuring him that this was not the end of the line.

"Sure I will," he agreed. "As for trust, I am the one who broke our trust first, by blowing up our lives and not even talking to you about it. I didn't want to talk with you about it, probably because I knew that if I said out loud what I was thinking, my greed and selfishness would be obvious even to me, and I couldn't bear that, let alone whatever valid but harsh things you would have to say about it. So,

I stayed stubborn and hoped it would all work out. I did not pay enough attention to you to see how much it was not working out. I am sorry for all of it, Gail."

Gail rose from her chair and went to perch on the arm of Jacob's. He put his arm around her waist and pulled her close. He might be thinner and frailer than before these attacks, but his big hands still felt reassuring. She rested her head on his, and they both closed their eyes for a moment. They had cleared the air and now they let it breathe, their years together weaving into a blanket of love and understanding that settled over them.

Riley meowed, ending the moment and making them both laugh. Gail sat up and rubbed her engagement ring with her right thumb.

"What do I do with all the things I bought? I can't return them," she said.

"Are you sure you can't wear them?" Jacob asked. "I bet you look good in them. Give me a fashion show." He waggled his eyebrows suggestively. Gail laughed.

"No, they are tainted for me."

"Okay, well, aren't you on the board of some charities? Could you auction them?"

"That is a great idea, Jacob! United Way has a fundraiser next month. I'll get in touch with the organizer and see if she wants them. At least the money will go to a good cause then, and the clothes and shoes and jewelry will make someone happy."

"There you go," Jacob said, squeezing her hand. "It will all work out."

Gail smiled down at him and squeezed his hand back.

"I think it will."

CHAPTER FORTY-SIX

Jacob had stopped talking to Gail about what to do when he died. He had tried his best with the conversation about the boat and the neighbor, and whether Nicole should name her child after him, and that had to be enough. It was too painful for Gail to talk about anymore.

Jacob did call Michael the day after that conversation, to ask him to take care of his estate when he was gone.

"I switched to that guy Shriver when you and I broke up," Jacob said, "but he's not nearly as good as you. I trust you to take care of my Gail and Nicole."

"I don't want to talk about this, Jacob, because I'm sure you're going to be okay," Michael said. "Still, as a fellow lawyer, I can't fault you for being prepared. I'll do it."

So now Jacob felt more secure, knowing that he had done everything he could to get his finances in good order and leave no loose ends for Gail to worry about when he was gone. He double-checked the finances after her revelation about her shopping sprees, but even with those considered, she was in good shape. He even had an envelope with funeral money in it, in among his will and other documents, so that she could pay cash and not stress about it.

He had always taken pride in being the breadwinner of the family and being able to provide. That pride carried over all the way through to his own death. He would take care of Gail until the very end, and even a little bit beyond it.

Despite having taken care of everything, or maybe because he had spent so much time thinking about his imminent death, Jacob could not shake himself out of the depression he had fallen into. Gail suggested he talk to Dr. Lowy about getting some medication for it, but Jacob insisted it would pass and he didn't need more drugs. Privately, he thought it was hardly worth it, as he would probably be dead before he even got the right dosage to help. Why waste the meds on him when another person could make use of them?

One evening, Gail and Jacob had just finished dinner, and Jacob was sitting in his chair with Riley in his lap while Gail cleaned up. He heard her in the kitchen, stacking plates in the dishwasher, running the pan under water. These domestic sounds soothed him. They meant he was still here, that the world still turned in the predictable way.

The doorbell rang, sounding very loud. Jacob called out in surprise, "Who's that?"

"I'll get it," Gail called from the kitchen. "It's Rabbi Eisel."

"What? Why didn't you tell me he was coming over?" Jacob asked.

"Because you would have said no," Gail said, passing through the living room on her way to the front door, wiping her hands on a dishcloth as she did so.

"He probably wants to get a jump on writing my eulogy," Jacob muttered to Riley. Riley looked at him askance and shoved his head under Jacob's hand. "Oh, I see you care a lot, huh. Thanks, pal," Jacob said in mock anger while obeying the cat's command and scratching behind his ears.

Gail returned to the living room, Rabbi Eisel in tow. Jacob started to rise, but the rabbi motioned for him to stay seated. Gail went back into the kitchen while the rabbi sat on the sofa by Jacob.

"How are you feeling?" he asked.

"Rabbi, how am I feeling? Frankly, I have been better," Jacob said wryly. "I can't go to work, and I have bills piling up. I'm doing my best, but my wife is watching my every move. If you have any pull upstairs, now would be a good time to make that call."

"God is watching, Jacob," the rabbi said. "Perhaps what I am about to propose may take your mind off things."

"Go ahead, Rabbi. I have all the time in the world to listen." Jacob checked himself. "No, actually, I am not in control of that either."

Rabbi Eisel smiled at this small display of humility from a man who used to pride himself on being proud. "You know that there is a women's prison in Chino?"

"Sure," said Jacob. "I've had clients there."

"Isn't that where the Manson girls are?" Gail asked from the kitchen.

"That's it," Jacob said.

"Well, a few years ago, I and another rabbi began offering women who were seeking spirituality an opportunity to study the Torah. And now, six years later, four of the women in our group have converted," the rabbi said.

"I didn't know. That's wonderful," Gail congratulated him.

"It is, praise God," the rabbi acknowledged. "One of the members, Laura, was given fifteen years to life. She has already served twenty-seven years."

At the name "Laura," Jacob saw a woman with long gray hair in his mind's eye. His hands started to shake. If the strange man with the dark eyes was a spirit, then surely Laura from the beach and the basketball game was one, too. This couldn't be the same one, though.

"For life!" Gail exclaimed. "What did she do?"

"She was convicted for conspiring to kill her husband," the rabbi said.

"Conspire? So, she didn't do it."

"Whether you actually commit the crime or act with someone to do the crime, if it results in death, you can be convicted of murder," Jacob clarified.

Gail shook her head at this as she returned from the kitchen, placing a cup of decaf and a bowl of nuts in front of the rabbi.

"I shouldn't eat these," Rabbi Eisel said, reaching for a handful of nuts. "I have to watch my salt intake."

"Well, you are not on a transplant list, so you should be okay," Jacob joked. Everyone laughed weakly.

"So, Rabbi, I'm confused," Jacob said. "How can I help?"

"Well, Laura has applied to the governor's office for clemency, which, if granted, would lead to her release," the rabbi said. "But there has to be a hearing first, and then a board makes a recommendation to the governor."

"I can't imagine how she managed twenty-seven years!" Gail said.

"She had an attorney," the rabbi continued, "but he died a few weeks ago. Very sudden. Terrible accident. Way too young. *Baruch dayan ha'emet.*"

Jacob let out a short bark of laughter. "Rabbi, I don't mean to be disrespectful, but are you suggesting that I take her case? Because, not to sound selfish, and I realize selfishness is probably why I am where I am today, but I just don't think I have the strength. And unless I get a new heart, she may be looking for a third attorney before her hearing."

"Jacob, with your knowledge I just thought that . . . " The rabbi took a sip of coffee and set the cup down. He looked into Jacob's eyes. "If you say yes, God will help you find the strength. From my mouth to God's ears."

Whether it was the same Laura who seemed to be a good spirit in his life or not, this woman was in need, and Jacob had to respond to that. He had put up a protest because he was genuinely exhausted and really did think he was going to die at any moment, but he no longer thought the way he used to—that it was all about looking out for number one and if they couldn't pay, they didn't deserve the time of day. He would help as much as he could, and that was all he could do.

"All right, Rabbi. I'll do it," Jacob said. Gail smiled. The rabbi grinned and shook his hand.

"Thank you, Jacob. That's good news. I'll set it up with the prison and let Laura know to expect you soon. We'll get you the paperwork from her last attorney's office."

"I guess we'd better clear this with Dr. Lowy too," Jacob said. "Looks like I'm back to work after all!"

CHAPTER FORTY-SEVEN

What a year for firsts and things from the past, Jacob thought. First heart attack and then another. Reconnecting with Michael. First grandchild on the way. And now today. It had been a long time since he had visited a prison. Here he was, in a prisoner meeting room, and nothing had changed. The windowless room was still painted a drab blue. The metal chair was still uncomfortable. It still felt like a place where hope came to die.

Rabbi Eisel placed his hands on the old wooden table in front of them and waited patiently. Jacob adjusted a setting on his oxygen tank. The door opened, and a female guard brought a woman in by the arm. The prisoner wore blue jeans and a denim shirt with a frayed collar. She held a book in her hand, which she placed on the table as she sat in the seat across from Jacob and the rabbi.

"You have thirty minutes," the guard informed them. "I'll be outside the door if you need me."

Jacob looked intently at Laura. She smiled at him, revealing a few

front teeth missing. As she smoothed the cover of the book in front
of her, he noticed her nails were bitten. Her face had the prematurely
old look of someone who had spent years in prison, but he thought
he recognized in it the woman from the beach those many months
ago. Besides, that long gray hair was distinctive.

"Hello, Laura," Rabbi Eisel said warmly. "This is Mr. Abrams, the
attorney I told you about. He is here to help you."

"Have we met?" Jacob asked. "I could swear that . . . "

Laura laughed. "I don't think so," she said. "I haven't left here in
twenty-seven years. But I guess it is possible, Mr. Abrams."

"I am going to step out," the rabbi said, rising to his feet.

Jacob said, "Please call me Jacob" as the rabbi slipped out the
door.

"All right. Jacob."

"Have you ever lived in Hawaii?" Jacob tried one more time.

"No, although I have dreamed of visiting. I do a lot of dreaming.
And they say everyone has a double."

Jacob was sure he'd heard that phrase before, too. He shook his
head at the coincidence and took out a yellow legal pad.

"I noticed the oxygen tank," Laura said. "The rabbi said you have
not been well?"

"Yeah," Jacob said. "Bad heart. And if they don't find me a donor,
well, I don't know how much time I have left."

"Ironic, isn't it," Laura said with a wry smile.

"How so?"

"I have an attorney who may lose his life while fighting to regain
mine," she mused. "Well, I guess God will see what kind of fighter
you are."

"I understand that you study the Torah with Rabbi Eisel," Jacob
said.

"Yes, I do," Laura said, patting the book in front of her. "Are you
a religious person?"

Jacob chuckled.

"What's so funny?" Laura asked warily.

"If someone had asked me that a year ago, I would have laughed in their face," Jacob said. "But now . . . "

"You don't believe in God?"

"I do. I mean, for a long time I did not. Not too long ago, it was as if"—he fumbled for the right words—"it was as if I got a message from God. And, well, anyway, you don't need to be bored by this."

"No, I want to hear," Laura said with interest, leaning forward, her gray hair catching the cold overhead light, reminding him of gray hair glowing in a sunrise.

"Are you sure we've never met?" he asked.

"Maybe spiritually," Laura suggested. "God has ways of bringing people together."

"Hmm. Maybe so," he conceded. Turning to business, he said, "Well, I looked at your file, and the parole board is about to set the date for your hearing. Hopefully that date comes soon because God sets my calendar."

CHAPTER FORTY-EIGHT

O ver the next two months, the spiritual journey that had begun for Jacob with a jolt to the heart continued in a small prison meeting room. He felt his body growing weaker, but he took comfort in the strength he found in talking with Laura. Although she was the prisoner, trapped behind walls, while he was free to come and go as he pleased, he felt trapped by mortality. His appointment with the executioner rapidly approached, and he sought spiritual guidance from this gentle woman who, while serving time, had all the time in the world. She seemed to thrive in this capacity, giving him counsel on how to live a better life and be a better man.

"What did you do before you started taking on pro bono cases?" Laura asked him at one of their first meetings.

"I was a criminal lawyer. Still am, or will be, if I get that heart transplant," Jacob replied.

"No, I mean, what charity did you do before?" she clarified.

"I did not do any charity at all before this past year, I'm ashamed to say," Jacob replied. "My wife would write checks, and sometimes we went to fancy charity dinners, but I saw those more as a networking opportunity, and a way to be seen, than as a way to help others."

"How were you spending your free time?"

"Oh, you know, wine, women, and song," Jacob joked. Laura smiled briefly but continued to stare at him. *She has the same lack of humor as the Laura on the beach, that's for sure,* Jacob thought.

"I bought a boat, and we went out on that whenever we could. I drove my fancy car really fast around the Canyon. I flirted with women but never actually cheated. I ate elaborate, expensive meals with my business partner and other lawyers. I tried taking up golf, but that is one boring game, I have to tell you."

"So, you spent all your time in pursuit of leisure, and a good portion of your money too, but no good works to balance it," Laura said.

"That's right," Jacob said. "Not the best approach, I know that now."

"No indeed."

———

On another visit, Laura asked him how much time he spent with his daughter.

"Nicole and I see each other quite a lot. Not as much now, because she's eight months pregnant and not feeling very mobile, and I pretty much don't leave the house anymore except to come here, but generally we see each other at least once a week."

"And who initiates that? Do you go to her house?"

"No, usually she comes to ours. That's fair, though, because then she can see her mother as well. It is her childhood home, you know."

"If she didn't visit you, would you visit her?"

"Yes, of course!"

"Has that always been true?"

Jacob thought for a moment. No, during the four years she was in college, he hardly ever saw her, because he kept working his long hours. And after that, when she and Aaron got married and Jacob fought with Michael, well, then he had not gone to her house because it was uncomfortable to see Aaron.

"No, I guess it has not. She's always had to make the effort," he admitted.

"It takes two people to maintain a relationship," Laura counseled.

"I know. We used to be closer when she was a kid. I wouldn't spend every day at the office past her bedtime, and sometimes I helped her with her homework. I always tried to go to her track meets, too. I haven't been the worst parent, you know," he said. He hated that he sounded defensive.

"Oh, I know," Laura said. "I'm just pointing out that it's easy to slip into bad habits. It's so easy for your sins to compound, and next thing you know, you can't remember the last time you saw your daughter or wrote a check for charity."

"Yes, I will keep that in mind."

———

At the end of their final meeting before the hearing, Jacob started packing up his attaché case.

"We're all set for Monday, and I think we have a really good shot at this," he said encouragingly.

"Thank you, Jacob," Laura said serenely. Jacob snapped his case closed and paused, his hand resting on the case.

"You know, I am really going to miss these. You've helped me prepare for, well," he stumbled.

"For what, Jacob? Dying?" Laura probed. "You *are* going to die if they don't find a heart. But we are all dying. Just some die sooner than others, and we have no control over any of it."

"I get it," Jacob said. "I just feel that if God is really listening . . . "

"God is always listening," Laura reminded him. "Listening and watching."

"Well, God must need glasses," Jacob grumbled, "because—oh, I don't know. Maybe I am a real screw-off."

"That's your problem," Laura said. "You can't *try* to be a good person. You have to *be* a good person. And just because you gave someone some money or showed some kindness, or even because you asked for forgiveness, that doesn't mean you are now cleansed of your sins."

Jacob nodded. She said this often, and each time, Jacob felt that he came closer to understanding and believing it.

Laura opened the book she carried with her everywhere. "The Torah talks about *teshuva*, or repentance. But that is only a blueprint to a better life. It is no guarantee of a long life."

Jacob stared at the wall, tears in his eyes. It was so hard to hear, and to accept.

"Jacob," Laura said, more gently now. "We make a living by what we get. But we make a life by what we give."

"That is very true," Jacob agreed.

"Well, I can't take credit for it; someone more famous than I said it. And although we can redeem ourselves through good acts, anything can still happen at any time, whether you are good or bad. Because in the final analysis, we have no control over the outcome of our lives and the results of our actions."

"I get it," Jacob said, a little defensively.

"Do you?" Laura wondered. "You've told me your worst attribute is your desire to be more important than others. Well, let me break it down, Jacob. You think your shit doesn't stink! But guess what? It does. And you have been stinking up the lives of all the people who love you." The tears in Jacob's eyes welled over.

"You want to appear the strong-willed person," Laura continued, "but you're weak. Because a person of humility will give of his time or money and be kind and not fear the consequences that might happen for making such a sacrifice. But the person who is always too busy and who never gives a few minutes of his time to the people in need, or is more concerned with growing his material wealth, is afraid of wasting his time, falsely believing that he has control over his life."

Jacob's tears flowed down his cheeks. He was so very sorry for who he had been, and exceedingly grateful to this woman for helping him see how he could be better. He so wanted to be.

Laura grabbed his hand and said urgently, "Jacob, God could have already taken you. But he did not. There is still time. But he needs to hear your confession."

CHAPTER FORTY-NINE

The next Monday, Jacob and Laura sat at a table in the hearing room of the prison. A framed photo of the governor was the only decoration on the far wall. Before them sat the hearing commissioner, with a microphone on a table in front of him. About ten feet away from Jacob and Laura, the attorney for the state went over his notes. A stenographer sat to the far right of the commissioner's table, fingers at the ready over her machine.

It had been a long while since Jacob had been well enough to be in a courtroom. This setup was familiar, and that familiarity comforted him. He was confident here. He turned to Laura and smiled encouragingly. She gazed back, unsmiling but serene.

"Good morning, Mr. Abrams, Mr. Jones," the commissioner began. The lawyers wished him a good morning. "Mr. Abrams, let the record reflect that we are in receipt of your suitability for clemency brief, the psychological and counseling report, as well as four letters of recommendation. Is there anything else that you wish to submit at this time?"

"No sir," Jacob replied into the microphone on his table. The commissioner pointed to the stenographer, indicating she should start up.

"Very well. We will mark these as exhibits F1 through F6. Let's go on the record." He straightened the paper in front of him, reading out, "This request for clemency is in the matter of Laura Ventro, case number CDC464616. Present in the room is Mr. Jones representing the people and Ms. Ventro along with her attorney. Counsel, please give your name for the record."

"Jacob Abrams."

"Thank you, Mr. Abrams," the commissioner said. "For the record, Ms. Ventro was convicted of 182 of the Penal Code and was sentenced to 15 years to life, of which she has served 27.4 years. Further, Ms. Ventro first became eligible for parole on 3/1/99, at which time a hearing was held and her request was denied. Subsequently on 6/2/2009, a second parole hearing was heard and that request was denied. She has now requested a clemency hearing. This commission, within 120 days of today and based on my finding, will submit my recommendation to the governor, who will then decide whether or not to issue a clemency order."

The only sound in the room other than the commissioner's voice was the tapping of the stenographer's machine and the wheezing of Jacob's oxygen tank.

"Further," the commissioner continued, "let the record reflect that, in mitigation, during the time of her incarceration, Ms. Ventro has been an exemplary prisoner. She has maintained employment in our library, and she has obtained her baccalaureate degree. However, in aggravation, she has shown no remorse for the crime she was convicted for and maintains her innocence. Does that adequately summarize the facts, Mr. Abrams?"

"Yes, it does," Jacob affirmed.

"Very well, you may proceed with your opening statement."

Jacob began to read from his prepared notes. "My client appears before you today, seeking that her sentence be commuted to time served. In support of our petition—" Pain seized Jacob's chest. He held a hand to his chest and tried to continue. "In support of our petition and upon your review, exhibits F3 through F6 contain letters of recommendation from—" Jacob stopped again. "Mr. Commissioner, one moment, please."

Jacob started frantically looking through his attaché case for his nitroglycerine pills. The commissioner shifted impatiently. Jacob glanced to his left and saw to his horror that the state attorney, previously sporting a short haircut, now had long black hair, and a cleft chin. The stranger's eyes were hooded as ever, but he started to laugh and held out his hand to Jacob.

"No, please," Jacob said under his breath.

"Mr. Abrams, did you say something?" the commissioner asked.

Jacob looked again to his left, but the state attorney was now himself again, looking at Jacob with concern.

"Yes. I mean, no," Jacob said. "I am sorry." He poured himself a glass of water with shaking hands and put a pill under his tongue. "I am ready to continue."

"Proceed."

Jacob returned to his prepared notes, but the pain in his chest intensified and his vision blurred. He rubbed his eyes to focus, but now he saw that the hearing room had changed. The walls were a bright white, and the governor's picture was gone. The commissioner was wearing a white suit, and the stranger had again taken the state attorney's place. The stranger reached out to Jacob and rose from his seat.

As the stranger stalked toward him, Jacob felt frightened, but he also heard the rabbi's words in his mind, from the class on Proverbs 6:16: "In some cases, the sinner has to bear the ultimate punishment decided upon by the tribunal." If this was it, so be it.

And then he felt Laura's hand on his arm. The tightness in his chest started to ease into a dull throb. The stranger returned to his seat and became the state attorney once more. Jacob turned to look at Laura and saw she was bathed in a golden glow. She smiled at him.

"I am ready," Jacob said.

"Proceed," the commissioner repeated.

Jacob set aside his legal pad and began to speak, without notes or plan, but with purpose and sincerity. "Clemency means the forgiveness of a crime. I am, ah, my client is here today asking for your forgiveness. But one cannot simply ask for forgiveness without explaining why. Twenty-seven years ago, my client was sentenced to fifteen years to life. When her appeals were gone, and she took those first steps inside her cell, a trapdoor opened beneath her, and she began a free fall that took her farther and farther away from the life that she once knew: the material things, the designer clothes, the fast life; speeding through every stop sign of life, never yielding long enough to notice who got hurt along the way.

"And then Laura crashed. And gone was her confidence and self-esteem. Gone was her smile. Gone was her hard work and the successes that she had already achieved, and her dreams for the future. Gone were the comforts and pleasures of her daily life. My—I mean, her—world had now become the size of her prison cell. She was no longer able to take in any of the simple beauties that were present around her.

"Her sight was clouded with fear and loneliness. And though she had visits from her family and friends at first, those visits decreased as the years passed. It is not that anyone ever gave up on their unwavering belief of her innocence. But the passage of time has a way of blurring the past. But one thing she never gave up on was that she still had a life. And she realized to survive, she needed to find a balance and reconnect with her true self. So, she made an important decision. She recognized that even though she was in prison, she would lead a full and joyous life. She had become almost one dimensional, and that was not healthy. She was more than a wrongly incarcerated woman. So, while continuing to fight for her freedom, she wanted to arrive at freedom a vibrant, happy, and loving woman."

Laura reached for Jacob's hand and covered it with her own. "Talk to God," she said softly, nodding toward the commissioner. Jacob wasn't sure where the lines of reality were blurring, but he felt the importance of this moment, so whether the commissioner was really God or whether he was a human who would think Jacob had lost it, he was taking this chance.

"What we do for ourselves dies with us. What we do for others and the world is and remains immortal," Jacob said. He chose his words with care. "But to do for others, I needed to first take an introspective look at myself. What value could I still bring to fulfilling my life and the lives of others? And what did I not have that you cannot buy nor quantify? Time. So, I started spending the time I had healing those around me. I volunteered my professional time. I have also taken full responsibility for the mistakes that I have made and the people that I have hurt.

"In my studies, the Talmud says that we must accept responsibility for our choices. Only then can we fully receive the forgiveness our heart needs to heal. I accept responsibility. But my heart cannot heal without you. What you see before you is a man of valor, of strength not weakness. A selfless man—or as close as I can get. And now, I ask for your forgiveness. But I cannot prove more of what I am capable of without you. I need your help. Give me the power to continue to heal the world."

CHAPTER FIFTY

A few days after Laura's hearing, Jacob attended another major event: his grandson's bris. Eight days after the baby was born, family and friends gathered at Jacob and Gail's for the ritual and celebration. Jacob felt extremely weak, but he visited Laker for a long heart-to-heart and returned to the house determined not to show it, to keep the focus on Nicole, Aaron, and the baby. If anyone asked, he would confirm that yes, he was still on the transplant list for a new heart, but he wouldn't bring it up himself.

He was immensely grateful that he had survived long enough to meet the baby. This perfect baby, from his own child, Nicole; this baby who almost didn't come into being due to Jacob's own selfish behavior. He knew that every time he saw his grandson, he would be reminded that a person's actions always affected others. *Even if we do not know how*, he thought.

Gail and Jacob greeted the guests alongside Michael and Diane, and Nicole and Aaron stood proudly in the living room, showing off their baby. The baby was dressed in a pale-blue smock and a yarmulke, and he was just about the most beautiful thing Jacob had ever seen. He had been born only days ago, but already Jacob and Gail had had many happy arguments over whether his nose or his chin were more like Nicole's.

When everyone had arrived, the mohel indicated that Jacob should sit. Jacob placed a pillow on his lap, and Nicole carefully laid her baby on the pillow. She joined Gail and Diane in the kitchen, as they did not want to watch. Other guests who didn't want to see the ritual milled about in the kitchen and backyard.

"Ladies and gentlemen," the mohel began, "I welcome you to this honored tradition. For the faint of heart, those who choose not to look, that's fine. But if you want to see an example of how good my work is, ask Aaron, as I was his mohel twenty-seven years ago."

Everyone laughed, and Aaron blushed as his father clapped a hand on his shoulder. The mohel poured a drop of grape juice on a square of cotton and placed it in the baby's mouth to quiet him. He recited a prayer, first in Hebrew and then in English.

"*anhnv mvknym lbts'e at mtsvvt bryt mylh lbhyvb, apylv kbvra, brvk hva, yhvh tsyvvh 'elynv, kmv shktvb bhvq, vhva shhva bn shmvnh ymym yhyh nymvl bynykm, kl dvr vdvr bkl zkr shlk dvrvt.* We are ready to perform the affirmative precept to the circumcision, even as the Creator, blessed be he, hath commanded us, as it is written, in the law, 'and he that is eight days old shall be circumcised among you, every male throughout your generations.'"

Jacob tried to stop it, but his legs began to shake.

The mohel joked, "I am good but not that good. So, if you want your grandson to end up with a nice-looking schmekel, I need you to relax."

The group laughed again. Not that long ago, Jacob would have been enraged that someone spoke to him like that, especially in front of other people. But now, he just smiled humbly. He took a deep breath and gazed down at his grandson, focusing on his perfect little face. His legs stilled.

And the next thing he knew, the mohel had done the deed, the baby was crying, and everyone was applauding. Nicole rushed into the room to take the baby, and Jacob slowly got to his feet. They all moved into the backyard, and Jacob met Rabbi Eisel at the drinks table.

"Jacob, mazel tov!" the rabbi said. "Can I get you something?"

Jacob grabbed a sparkling water. "Rabbi, remember *The Wizard of Oz*?"

"Of course." The rabbi nodded.

"Well, tell me you're the wizard, and I will ask you for a heart," Jacob said with a crooked smile.

The rabbi put a reassuring hand on Jacob's arm and said, "Jacob, you are not a tin man but a very strong man. I know you will hear something soon."

———

Two weeks later, the rabbi was repeating these words, this time in a hospital room while standing next to Gail and Nicole. Jacob had grown too weak. He lay in the hospital bed with an oxygen mask over his face, which made it difficult to talk. He mostly smiled at visitors and feebly squeezed their hands in thanks. Visiting hours were nearly over, and the nurses dimmed the lights; the only bright light in the room came from the EKG monitor flashing over Jacob's head. The rabbi finished up, kissed Jacob on the forehead, and left.

"I must be near the end," Jacob rasped to Gail. "Rabbi Eisel has never kissed me on the forehead." Gail smiled with tears in her eyes. "It's late, Nicole," Jacob continued. "You should be with my beautiful grandson."

"Dylan is fine, Dad," Nicole said. "Aaron and his parents are with him. I want to be here with you." She choked on the last few words and stifled a sob.

Jacob removed his oxygen mask to see his beloved wife and daughter more clearly.

"I had a good run, didn't I?" he asked. Gail clutched his hand, and Nicole put her arm around her mother. "I really tried." He wanted them to know that.

"Close your eyes. Rest," Gail urged.

"I think I will. You guys go home. I'll see you in the morning," Jacob said sleepily.

"I love you, Dad," Nicole said through tears.

"I love you, sweetheart," Jacob replied. Nicole gave him a kiss on the cheek.

"Jacob, I'm just going to walk Nicole out, but I am coming right back," Gail said. Jacob weakly raised his hand to say okay, and then closed his eyes.

Moments later, he felt the touch of a warm hand on his. He opened his eyes to see a curtain of gray hair, and then he focused on the face of Laura, glowing as she had been in Hawaii. He was dimly aware that the EKG monitor beeping was slowing.

"Laura," Jacob said, without fear. "So, how does it work? Do I just get out of bed and follow you?"

Laura laughed. "You have seen too many movies, Jacob. And no, it is not yet time. In fact, God sent me here to bring you a message."

As he opened his mouth to reply, Gail returned to the room.

"Who are you talking to?" she asked him.

"Laura. She's here," Jacob said.

"Jacob, no one else is here," Gail said slowly.

"No, she is," Jacob insisted, pointing next to him, where Laura smiled beatifically.

Before they could argue further about it, Dr. Lowy burst into the room, a grin on his face.

"Jacob! Gail!" he exclaimed. "Have I got good news for you! Let's scrub you up, Jacob. You're getting a new heart."

Gail shrieked and hugged Dr. Lowy. Jacob turned to Laura, who squeezed his hand. "I'll be right here," she reassured him. "You are getting your second chance."

CHAPTER FIFTY-ONE

Gail ran a finger down her grandson's cheek and felt her heart swell. She'd never thought she could love another tiny creature the way she had loved Nicole when she first held her in her arms, but the first time she met Henry, she felt the same sense of overwhelming protectiveness and awe. Maybe it was because he came from Nicole, maybe it was simply the biological imperative required for people to care for helpless babies, but whatever it was, Gail was in love with this child, from his tiny bald head down to his little sausage toes. He had Nicole's nose (not her chin—what was Jacob thinking?), and Aaron's eyes. He was the bright spot in all their lives.

Dr. Lowy came out of the surgery, where he had been observing the surgeon. Gail sat up straighter, keeping a gentle hand on her grandson's forehead. She felt Nicole stiffen beside her as well.

"It went great," he said before he even reached them. They both relaxed visibly. "The surgeon is satisfied with how the procedure went. But Jacob needs to recover now, and it is going to take some time. He is not going to be out of here tonight, and maybe not even tomorrow night. You will not be able to see him until early morning, so if you want to go home and get some rest, that might be a good idea."

They thanked him profusely, and then turned to one another to discuss next steps. Nicole wanted to stay longer, but Gail insisted that she go home. She was a new mother, and both she and the baby were exhausted. Let her go home and have Aaron take care of them both. Nicole eventually agreed, and after a fierce hug with her daughter and a lingering kiss on her grandson's forehead, Gail waved them out.

She settled back in the hard waiting room chair and smoothed her hair behind her ears. She was tired, but she was not going home tonight. She would stay here until they let her see him. The thought of going back to their big house and trying to sleep on her own made her shiver. Even with Riley there for comfort, she would feel so alone and afraid. No, better to be here in this uncomfortable chair, in this rather cold room with the harsh lighting, than back in the comfort of her home. Here, she could be closer to Jacob. That was all that mattered to her right now.

They had nearly lost each other there, in the communication breakdown of the last few years. They had found each other again before it was too late. They were going to be stronger than ever now, and she was not going to miss a moment of it.

———

Nicole held her son to her chest. She was exhausted in every way, physically, emotionally, and mentally. Henry had been born with no complications, thank goodness, but labor was still an incredibly stressful experience, and her body was in recovery. At the same time, her new son needed all her attention. He took to breastfeeding easily, which was a relief because this was not always the case and Nicole had, in true worrier fashion, been anxious about how she would cope with that if she needed to. But he was either sleeping or crying or eating or pooping, and Nicole had to be there for all of it. Aaron helped as much as he could, and she didn't know what she would do without him. It was a good thing they had planned for him to take a full month off of work when the baby was born (and how grateful she was that they could afford the time off). They were going to need all that time to get used to keeping this tiny life alive.

But all this wonderful new life came at a time that they all feared secretly (but never said out loud) might be the end of another life. Jacob hadn't had another attack, but he had grown weaker and weaker, until there was no recourse but to put him in the hospital. Just as they had all started to face the harsh reality that he might not leave the hospital alive, Dr. Lowy burst in with his miraculous news. A donor! Nicole sent fervent prayers of thanks, as well as prayers of healing to the family who had to lose one of their own for Nicole's dad to have a second chance.

Henry started crying, and Nicole helped him suckle. Aaron called out from the other room, "Do you want some water, hon?"

"Yes please," she called back.

They were in a holding pattern now that the surgery had gone well, and Gail had insisted that Nicole go home.

"Go take care of our grandson so he's healthy and happy when your father wakes up," Gail had said.

Nicole hugged her hard and whispered, "He is going to wake up, Mom. I think this time he's really going to turn the corner. I can feel it."

"I feel it too, sweetheart. It's been quite a ride, but I think we're coming to the light at the end of the tunnel."

Aaron appeared in the doorway, a glass of water in one hand and a sandwich in the other.

"I don't think you've eaten in a few hours, is that right?" he asked. "Here, eat this."

"I have never been more in love with you than I am now," Nicole said gratefully.

"Hey, I thought it might have been when I gave you that huge engagement ring or took you on that expensive honeymoon. If I had known all I needed to do was make a sandwich, I'd be a much richer man!" They both laughed.

"You know you are about as rich as a man can get," Nicole said.

Aaron looked down at his wife, glowing in the warm bedroom light, and their tiny child suckling at her breast.

"Oh, I know."

————

The next morning, a nurse shook Gail gently awake and asked her if she would like to get some breakfast before she saw Jacob.

"The doctor will probably let you see him in about half an hour," she said as Gail wiped the sleep from her eyes. "I thought you might want a coffee or something before that."

"Thank you, I think I will do that," Gail said. *There are so many kind people in the world*, she thought as she went down to the cafeteria. So many people who took the extra step to help another person. She saw it more and more lately. It was like a veil had been lifted, and before where she saw only her husband's petty actions and her own petty reactions, she now remembered there was so much more. It was like their honesty with one another had opened the world again.

The doctor gave her the usual warning that Jacob was in recovery and she must be quiet and not stay too long. She nodded in agreement; this was all familiar to her, but she tried not to be impatient.

In the room, she ducked behind the privacy curtain drawn around her husband's bed. Jacob was propped up on pillows, sipping on a juice cup. When he saw Gail, his face broke into a giant grin.

"Gail!" he exclaimed.

"Oh, Jacob," she said, rushing to his side and reaching down to envelop him in a hug. He stroked the back of her head as she let out a little sob of relief.

"Oh, my love, I have never been so happy to see someone in my whole life," he murmured.

"I feel the same," she said.

"And I think I have quite a bit more life in me," he said. Gail pulled back and looked at him, saw the serious, peaceful look on his face.

"I think so too," she replied. "A new heart, a new start."

"That's right. Or maybe I even made a new start, and I earned a new heart."

"Well, whatever it is, you have it now, and it's going to make a huge difference. We will stay on the heart-healthy foods, you will not smoke anymore, and you can start walking again."

"Yes, it's the total lifestyle change that Lowy said I had to make, all that time ago," Jacob agreed. "I wonder what would have happened if I had listened to him? What if I had read that book he prescribed sooner? Would it have made a difference?"

"That's all in the past and moot now," Gail said. "You're here, and you're going to recover and get healthy. We are going to have the life we want together, with our friends, our daughter and son-in-law, and our beautiful grandson. That's what you can do with your what-if!"

They both laughed and then leaned in for a kiss that seemed to hold within it all the possibilities of the years ahead.

CHAPTER FIFTY-TWO
One year later

Jacob and Gail's house was once again the site for a celebration, but this time no shadow of ill health fell over the party. Jacob was celebrating one year with his new heart, and his grandson was celebrating one year on this earth. The skies were blue, and Jacob's heart was light.

Jacob stood at the barbecue, grilling turkey burgers and smiling at his blessings. He no longer needed an oxygen tank, and his clothes fit right again. He was slimmer than he had been before his first heart attack, but it was a healthy weight loss, not like the wasting away before his heart transplant. He had returned to work part time, and though they were still no longer partners, he and Michael often shared business and helped each other out.

The two couples and their children had been out on the boat a few times already, and Jacob eagerly awaited the day Nicole would say it was okay for Henry to join. He and Gail saw Henry often, and it was still a surprise to Jacob how much fun it was to spend time with a baby. He'd loved Nicole when she was born, of course, but he hadn't done any of the caretaking—too busy making money in those long-ago days when he thought that was important. He knew better now.

The radio next to the grill was tuned to the Lakers game, and Jacob was cheering Kobe through another three-pointer when Nicole walked over, carrying Henry. Jacob immediately reached out for his grandson and admired the Lakers jersey he was wearing.

"You say that every time you see him in that jersey, Dad," Nicole said, smiling indulgently. Jacob swung Henry into the air and listened to him giggle.

"I do?" Jacob said with a grin.

"You're the one who got it for him! You're impossible," she said. They laughed together.

Smoke began billowing out of the barbecue.

"Don't burn them, Dad," Nicole warned. She reached out for Henry, and Jacob quickly adjusted the cover of the grill. Nicole leaned over and gave Jacob a hug with her free arm.

"I love you, Dad."

Jacob kissed her on the forehead. "You are my precious angel," he whispered. Nicole smiled and joined Aaron at the table.

Jacob flipped the burgers as the smoke dissipated. When he looked up, he saw Laura in front of him, wearing a pale-green pantsuit and appearing younger than she had in prison.

"Laura!" Jacob exclaimed warmly. She smiled. "I didn't know. Last time I checked, the governor was still dragging his feet. When did you . . . ?"

"Two weeks," Laura said. "He finally signed the order, and here I am."

"So, what are you going to do?" Jacob asked, putting down the burger tongs and wiping his hands on his apron.

"Well, first I am going to get my teeth fixed," Laura said with some embarrassment. "And then, well, we'll see. But I wanted to come by and say thank you."

"No," Jacob said, "I am the one who needs to say thank you."

"You gave me my life back," Laura reminded him.

"And you helped me find mine!" Jacob insisted. There was a moment of silence as they gazed at each other with the affection and respect of two people who had been through a harrowing journey together. Jacob thought this must be what it was like to see a war buddy years after the trenches.

"Well, you look great," Laura said finally.

"I feel great," Jacob affirmed, and he was thrilled to feel how true that was.

"You are going to be here a long time," Laura promised.

"I will?" Jacob asked, raising his eyebrows.

"Yeah. I got the email," Laura joked. They both laughed.

But Jacob couldn't let this moment pass without acknowledging something. "You really are my guardi—" He stopped as Laura put her hand to her lips.

"I just came by to say hello," she said simply.

It was suddenly difficult to see her as smoke poured out of the grill again, obscuring everything but her long gray hair. Jacob lifted the cover, saying, "No, please stay. I want you to meet Gail." But by the time he closed the lid, Laura had disappeared.

Well, that was how it had always been between them. He was just grateful to have seen her at all.

Gail meandered over from the table. "How are things over here?" she asked, poking at the burgers with the tongs.

Jacob playfully pushed her aside. "Hey, I'm in charge here! Didn't you hear? I have a new heart, so I'm a big strong man again, and this is my barbecue!"

Gail laughed and kissed him on the lips. "My big strong man, indeed."

Jacob started piling burgers on a plate. "All right," he called to the party guests, "let's eat!"

As he closed the cover on the barbecue, Jacob heard the radio announce a last-minute basket in the game. "Score! And the Lakers move on to the playoffs!"

Jacob cheered, and everyone cheered with him. Jacob picked up a plate and glanced up at the sky. His heart had never been so full.

9 781646 636189